Readers Love

Rekindled Flame

"What a fantastic, multilayered, and emotionally moving book!"

—Rainbow Book Reviews

Cleansing Flame

"I love Andrew Grey's writing… he does sweet romance in totally relatable, real life situations."

—MM Good Book Reviews

Smoldering Flame

"I am not one to reread a lot but this is on my will-read-again list!"

—TTC Books and More

Past His Defenses

"This story gives you exactly what you're looking for in a romance novel and it was the perfect escape from reality for just a little while."

— Love Bytes Reviews

Heartward

"Not only is it a book about finding a home but it is a book about finding a family."

— Gay Book Reviews

By Andrew Grey

Published by DREAMSPINNER PRESS
www.dreamspinnerpress.com

By ANDREW GREY (cont'd)

Published by DREAMSPINNER PRESS
www.dreamspinnerpress.com

By ANDREW GREY (cont'd)

Published by DREAMSPINNER PRESS
www.dreamspinnerpress.com

THROUGH the FLAMES
ANDREW GREY

DREAMSPINNER PRESS

Published by
DREAMSPINNER PRESS

8219 Woodville Hwy #1245
Woodville, FL 32362 USA
www.dreamspinnerpress.com

Through the Flames
© 2024 Andrew Grey

Cover Art
© 2023 Melody Pond
https://melodyypond.weebly.com/
Cover content is for illustrative purposes only and any person depicted on the cover is a model.

Mass Market Paperback ISBN: 978-1-64405-855-8
Trade Paperback ISBN: 978-1-64108-466-6
Digital ISBN: 978-1-64108-465-9
Mass Market Paperback published February 2024
v. 1.0

Printed in the United States of America
∞
This paper meets the requirements of
ANSI/NISO Z39.48-1992 (Permanence of Paper).

*To Dominic, with all my love.
Thank you for letting me research
sexy firemen for inspiration.*

CHAPTER 1

IT HAD been said that the difference between love and hate could be measured as the width of a hair. Hayden Walters wasn't so sure.

"Going to bury yourself in a book, bookworm?" Jason Wilson asked. The man was a mountain of pain in the ass, and not in an "oh my God" good kind of way. But he wasn't as bad as his brother, Kyle, who had to be the biggest asshole on the planet. Maybe it was something in the water where they grew up.

Hayden gritted his teeth. "Do you actually think you're clever?" He had no idea what caused it, but those two had to be some of the worst human beings to have ever lived.

Okay, that was an exaggeration. Kyle was awful, sure, but part of Hayden's problem with Jason was hatred transference. Jason *could* be an ass, but no one at the station really paid that any attention.

Hayden could take their cue. He picked up his coffee mug to find more amenable company somewhere else. He refused to let the oaf's comments get to him. After all, Hayden had endured Kyle's bullying—including shoving him into lockers—his entire time in high school, so shit like that shouldn't get to him. Jason was nothing. Hell, Hayden didn't even know if Jason actually disliked him. He made up nicknames and teased everyone in the station.

"Knock it off, Wilson," Greg Luther said as he passed, clapping Hayden on the shoulder. Greg was the other gay firefighter in their fire company in Carlisle, Pennsylvania. He'd been part of the company for eight years, while Hayden had been hired on just a year and a half ago, fresh out of fire academy, but they only started working similar shifts a few months ago. "I know you think you're funny, but no one else does. What the hell happened to you? Your mama drop you on your head one too many times?"

"Look who thinks he's funny," Jason said.

"*You* certainly aren't." Hayden clenched his hands and left the room. Jason was an ass, but Hayden had found he was harmless—unlike his fucking brother, who could be lethal in his meanness. Maybe that was why he had such a hard time with Jason. The two men looked so alike it was uncanny, though Jason was older. Granted, so far Hayden hadn't found much to like about Jason either, but it wasn't like the guy was the antichrist… that would be Kyle. No, Hayden just needed to find a way to get along with the guy, and he had to remember that Jason wasn't his brother.

He figured he could find something to do to make himself useful out of the presence of the department clown. Hayden liked to be busy, and he wanted to make himself as productive as possible. As one of the newest members of the fire company, he still had plenty to prove, and he strove to do that every chance he got. After all, if the other guys accepted him, maybe he could figure out a way to leave behind the small, skinny, never-fit-in-anywhere kid he'd once been. He was no longer skinny, with impressively broad shoulders and a muscled chest, but that misfit kid was still inside him.

Before he could find something to do, the fire alarm blared, and everyone sprang to life. Hayden suited up as the details of the call came in. House fire on Pomfret. Union was responding and requested backup.

There were two fire companies in Carlisle. Union Fire Company was right downtown. They were also the oldest and the one with the local fire equipment museum in the old part of their facility. Carlisle Fire and Rescue was on the north side of town in a new facility. If Union was requesting backup this fast, it had to be a bad one.

Hayden climbed on the truck and took his place in the back of the cab. He held on as they screamed out of the drive and made the left turn onto Spring Road, racing toward the fire.

Lights changed color ahead of them, bringing traffic through the historic district of downtown to a halt. Hayden barely noticed the old courthouse with its clock tower and Civil War scars as they zoomed past and then made the right turn onto Pomfret, heading down the block and a half to where the other company was already setting up.

"Wet down roofs, make sure the fire doesn't spread to the other row houses," Union's chief called almost as soon as they came to a stop. "It's a bad one and growing hotter in the old house."

Breaking glass pulled Hayden's attention, and movement from behind the now fully open upstairs window caught his attention.

"There's someone in there," Hayden said.

"We were told it was empty," the Union chief said as Hayden hefted on his breathing gear.

"Go, but don't take long, for God's sake. The back of the building is where the fire started, probably in the kitchen. Stay to the front," Greg, the fire captain for their unit, told him. He had the ability to read a fire like few others, and Hayden expected him to be chief someday.

"Got it." His mind was already inside.

"The staircase is going to be right in front of you when you enter. Get up, find whoever is in there, and get the hell out fast. Don't linger," Greg told him.

Hayden pulled on his mask and started the flow of air as he raced for the door. He immediately stepped into a thick gray fog of swirling smoke, the stairs looming out of it. Glass broke behind him, but he paid little attention. It was probably the guys knocking out the windows so they could get water on the blaze.

As he reached the top of the stairs, flames shot skyward through the back of the house. What had once been a bedroom was now an inferno, and a portion of the floor had collapsed. The guys were going to have a hard time getting resources to that part of the building, but judging by the hissing that accompanied the roar of flame, they were trying their best. Picking up the pace, Hayden hurried forward. He checked the old bathroom and then the first bedroom he came to, which was empty. He closed the door and went forward to where he thought he'd seen movement.

A man lay on the floor. Hayden wasn't sure if he was still alive. Hayden pulled him up and hefted him over his shoulders, then started back toward the stairs. The fire was now running along the ceiling over his head, consuming the old horsehair plaster at a rapid pace, embers and ash falling all around him. Hayden's heart raced, but he kept his head even when he was no longer able to see.

Using his hands, he found the top of the banister, and then his foot found the first step. He didn't dare turn around, knowing the wall of fire behind him was consuming the house like a ravenous wolf. He had to get out before everything collapsed around both of them.

One step at a time, he descended, growing closer to the door. Flames jumped up to the side on the first floor, and the entire staircase shuddered as he got lower. Hayden could almost feel the building giving up under the onslaught. Three more steps and large pieces of ceiling collapsed around him, sending up more ash, feeding the flames that flared even higher. Two more steps and the staircase shook like hell. Hayden realized he only had a matter of seconds. He reached the last few steps and jumped to the floor, making for the front door with a last burst of energy as everything behind him collapsed in a conflagration, propelling Hayden and his charge out through the doorway. He would have crashed to the ground if two other firefighters hadn't caught them both.

Together, they got the man away from the building and onto a gurney, where an EMT immediately took over. Hayden continued away from the collapsing row home, pulled off his breathing gear, and sucked in beloved fresh air. Once he made it to the truck, he took off his fire coat and let the spring air get to his shirt, now plastered to his skin by sweat.

"You did good," Greg told him. "Fucking damn good."

"Is he alive?" Hayden asked. Right now, it was the only thing important to him.

"They're still working on him." Greg turned away to give more orders. "Keep spraying the home next door. I don't want to lose it now… good." Greg hurried away, and Hayden grabbed a bottle of water and sucked it down. Then he pulled his coat back on, donned his hat, and joined the rest of the men helping to get this beast of a fire out.

He manned a hose, trying to get to the heart of the fire. Their current jobs were to prevent the fire from spreading to the neighboring homes and keep the side walls from collapsing under all the strain from the heat. They were going to be weakened, that was certain, but if they gave way, the buildings on either side would be unlivable and additional families would find themselves without a home. Hayden aimed his stream of water through one of the front windows, sending it cascading through the building. They were finally making headway. A large part of the back roof was gone, but the flames had died considerably, and within an hour the chief declared the fire out.

The police had shown up, and they took over securing the exterior of the building and directing traffic around where they were working.

"Hey, Red," Greg said as he shook Red's hand.

"You guys had a big one," Red commented.

"Yeah. We're going to check out the buildings on either side. I suspect they'll need new roofs, and there's likely to be water damage." Greg directed some of the men to begin winding up the hoses.

Hayden turned off the water, and once Jason signaled that the pressure was off, he turned the hose on to bleed the water out—but the unexpected force nearly knocked him onto his butt.

"Very funny," Hayden called as the pressure bled away.

"Knock it off, Jason," Greg admonished and stalked right up to him. "This is work, not a circus. If you can't act like a professional and stop playing your games, I'm going to ask the chief to reevaluate your position here. Am I making myself clear?"

Jason scoffed. "What? I thought it was off." He clearly knew different. "Can't guys like you take a joke?"

Greg didn't back down. "Get your ass on the truck now. That's harassment, and you know it won't be tolerated. At the very least, you're going to have to do the sensitivity training… again. Maybe this time you won't sleep through it." Greg was angry, and Hayden didn't blame him. He wanted to take Jason's head off himself.

"I heard what he said," Red said as he stood behind Greg, arms folded over his chest.

For the first time since Hayden joined the company, Jason seemed to grow smaller. "It was just a joke, nothing more." He took a step back, lowering his gaze slightly. "You did good getting the man out of the building." That was Jason-speak for an apology, because he wasn't likely to compliment anyone for another reason.

"Thanks." Hayden drained his hose and started rolling it up.

"Hayden, let Jason do that. You go check on the man you rescued. They're about to transport him." Greg smiled as he gave Jason the crap job, and Hayden didn't argue, heading over to where the EMTs were loading the only person injured in the fire. That alone was some sort of miracle.

"How is he?" Hayden asked.

"He's breathing on his own now, and he's awake," Karen answered. She and Hayden had crossed paths a number of times before. She was something else. Even as far back as high school, Karen had always been an amazing person. They were in the same graduating class, but while she had been popular and outgoing, Hayden had done his best to try to blend in with the paint. "Come on, you can talk to him a minute before we take him in to be checked out. I'd say you got to him just in time." She led the way around the back of the ambulance, and Hayden followed and peered into the vehicle.

"I understand you saved me," the man said as Hayden stepped up. Hayden's breath hitched, and he blinked more than once. No way—this couldn't be right. "Thanks, man. You're a real hero." He smiled and Hayden nodded, forcing a smile as he stared into the dirty face of Kyle Wilson, Jason's brother and probably the one person on earth Hayden wished he could have simply left in the burning building. Not that he would have, but still.

"Glad I could help," Hayden mumbled and then stepped out and immediately turned away. "His brother, Jason, is one of the firefighters in my company. Does he know about Kyle?"

"Yeah. They had a gorilla-type chest-pounding argument a little while ago that the EMTs broke up."

She rolled her eyes. "They're both real pieces of work as far as I can tell, though that may be just how they are." She closed the back door of the ambulance, and Hayden backed away and returned to where they guys were cleaning up and getting ready to leave.

"Did you talk to him?" Greg asked.

"Yeah. I think the guy is going to be okay." Hayden didn't really want to talk. Greg was many things: a great captain, a super mentor… and a pain in the ass when he realized there was something he didn't know. "Did you know that was Jason's brother?"

Greg nodded. "It seems they don't get along anymore. They had a falling out. Jason used to talk about Kyle all the time. Apparently, Kyle was like Superman… and then something changed, and now they don't speak."

Hayden nodded but didn't say anything. When Greg didn't continue, Hayden returned to gathering up the last of their equipment. He stowed it and then climbed onto the truck for the ride back to the station. He'd done his job and saved one of the people he hated most in the world. Maybe that bit of karmic goodness would come back to him in a good way… or maybe it would bite him in the ass. Either way, at least he wasn't likely to see Kyle ever again—and he could live with that.

CHAPTER 2

"YOU DIDN'T burn down my house, did you?" Ellen asked earnestly but without heat, which was surprising. Lying in the hospital bed, breathing in oxygen, Kyle had wondered the same thing, but as far as he could recall, he had done nothing that could have started the fire.

Kyle rolled his head slowly. "No, I didn't." At least he didn't think so. His memory was a little fuzzy. Every time he tried to concentrate, his head spun and he ended up closing his eyes. The doctors said that would pass and told him to rest for a while. "You had me working in the front rooms, remember? I was repairing the plaster in the first two bedrooms. I had my ear buds in and didn't realize anything until smoke filled the room I was working in. The door to the room had been removed and was in the basement because you wanted it stripped." His throat was rough and still sore, but at least he was alive.

"So you weren't where the fire started?" Ellen had purchased the property maybe two months ago and had hired him to help her make the house livable for her and her two daughters. "I'm not sure what caused it, but they think it started in the kitchen."

"That's my guess, but I don't know. I tried to get out and broke the window to try to get breathable air, but it didn't work too well. The smoke just billowed out and the air rushed into the room from the rest of the house." The last thing he remembered was crouching on the floor, because that was where he was hoping for better air. His plan was to try to make it to the stairs, but he didn't get far. The smoke was too much. The next thing he knew, he'd come back to consciousness outside with EMTs all around him. "Apparently a firefighter went inside the house to get me and hauled me out."

"He did, yeah. And word around town is that he saved your life."

Kyle sat up but ended up coughing, and Ellen helped him back down onto the bed. "Sorry, and I'm sorry about your house too. It was going to be beautiful, I know that." He had already been working on the place for two weeks, and it had been starting to come together. Once the bedrooms were done, he had expected the new cabinets to arrive so he could put the kitchen together. After that, his next task would have been to tackle the bathrooms. He had expected another two months of solid work on the place, but now that was up in smoke right along with Ellen's house. "But I didn't start the fire." He coughed again and watched Ellen deflate.

"Thank God," she whispered. A questionable fire would delay an insurance payment.

"Was everything insured?" Kyle asked. He'd hate for her to lose everything she had. "I know you just bought the house and…." You needed insurance to get a mortgage, right?

"Yes, it was. That isn't an issue. The house was completely destroyed, and we'll need to figure out things with the insurance company, but I'm hoping we can start looking for a new home soon. But it will probably be weeks." She had troubles of her own, but so did Kyle. "I'm glad you're going to be okay and that the fire was accidental."

"Me too." It would be hard to live with himself if he knew he was at fault. "I really appreciate you stopping by to see me."

Ellen took his hand. "Has anyone else been up?"

Kyle had known Ellen for three years now. When she got the house she was in now, he had helped do the work she needed. Ellen had been one of his first clients when he'd decided to try contracting on his own.

"Jason was one of the firefighters at the house. He saw me and knows that I got out alive. I guess he'll tell anyone else who wants to know." He sighed and forced himself to relax. "When you find a house, you know I'll be there to help you with it."

Ellen smiled and patted his hand. "I know you will. I need you to put together your bill for all your work so I can get the insurance company to pay for it." He supposed if he had to in order to keep Ellen from getting screwed, they could say that it had all been in the house. "I'm hoping we can use what's on order in the new house."

"I'll do that just as soon as I get home." Breathing kept getting easier, and he closed his eyes. "When are you supposed to be out of your house?" She had already sold it, and they were waiting for closing.

"Another month. After that I'm not sure what I'll do. I could back out, but that would only complicate things even further."

Kyle nodded. "I could talk to my family." Even saying the words hurt. Yeah, he could try to contact them, but it didn't mean they'd take his call. "My parents have a house they rent out on the south side."

"No. You don't worry about us. We have friends who have offered us places to stay until we can figure things out. But we can rent if we have to." She took his hand. "Just get better and call me when you're on your feet again." Ellen stood up, leaned over the bed, and lightly kissed his cheek. Then she left the room, and Kyle relaxed, trying not to think about his breathing, because every time he did, he inhaled either too quickly or too deeply and started coughing once more. What he really needed was a job. He had turned down other work because he was going to be busy at Ellen's getting the house rehabbed, and now that was gone… along with his ability to breathe. Who knew how long that was going to keep him home.

Financially, he had a little bit of a cushion, and once he was on his feet, he could hopefully find some work to fill the time until his next bigger job, which was scheduled to a start in a few months. Kyle put all of that aside. There was nothing he could do about it in a hospital bed while they gave him oxygen and told him to rest so his lungs could heal. Maybe once he was home, he could figure all that out.

THERE WERE only two fire stations in town, and Kyle had tried Union first because they were the first unit to respond to the fire and because his brother worked at Carlisle Fire and Rescue, and he wanted to avoid him if possible.

"I don't know who it was. I wasn't on duty," the brick wall of a firefighter said before turning. "Lee, do you know who rescued the man from the home on Pomfret the other day?"

Another firefighter approached, this one equally as stunning as the first one. Together they oozed enough testosterone to nearly make Kyle drunk. "I think it was one of the guys from CFR. They arrived later, but one of their men saw the guy break a window and he charged right in." Lee's smile brightened a little as soon as he turned to the other man, and damned if the guy, as big as a house, didn't melt a little right there. Damn, Kyle wanted that so bad he could taste it. No one had to tell him that these guys were a couple. All they had to do was look at each other and Kyle knew it. Just a single look and that was it. Kyle pulled himself out of his moment of longing.

"Thanks."

"Why do you want to find him?" Lee asked.

Kyle coughed. "I'm the guy he rescued, and I wanted to thank him. I got out of the hospital a few days ago, and I really need to thank the guy. I kind of remember that he looked in on me when I was in the ambulance. I know he saved my life." He shook hands with both men. "I appreciate your help."

"You're welcome," the first man said. Kyle hadn't caught his name. Then he left the station and got into his car and headed out to the far north side of town.

Kyle pulled into the sizable parking lot and turned off the engine, but he stayed in the truck for a moment. He hoped his brother wasn't working today. He didn't need the stress of running into him. Maybe this wasn't such a good idea after all. He could just go home and write a note and send it to the station.

"Yeah, that's the chickenshit way out," he told himself and got out of the truck. He still coughed if he breathed too quickly, but it was getting better every day. Hopefully in another week he could go back to work.

In the reception area, a man sat behind a plastic window, typing on a computer. "Can I help you?" he asked as he continued typing.

"Yeah, I…. That fire the other day on Pomfret."

The man nodded. "Yeah, I'm told that was a bad one."

Kyle nodded. "It was, I guess. I was the guy that was rescued, and I wanted to thank the man who went in and got me. He saved my life, and I wanted to thank him. I don't know his name, and I only saw him briefly before they took me to the hospital. I'm told it was one of the guys from here who got me."

"Sure. Let me look," he said, typing away. "Yeah. It was Hayden, and I think…." He grabbed a sheet of paper. "Yeah, he's on shift today. Let me check and see if I can find him." He stood and left the small office area and hurried out.

Kyle sat in one of the chairs nearby and did his best to relax. The doctors said he needed to stay calm, and he didn't know why he was nerved up.

Kyle remembered the face of the guy in the ambulance. He seemed nice enough.

"He'll be right out," the man said from inside the window. Then the typing began again, and Kyle settled into his seat.

A few minutes later, the door from the back opened and a man with broad shoulders stepped out like he was ready to go into battle. His eyes were hard and his body straight and rigid.

"I'm Kyle Wilson. You probably work with my brother, Jason—" He began to cough and covered his mouth with his hand. "Sorry." He cleared his throat. "I understand you pulled me out of the fire on Pomfret."

Hayden narrowed his gaze and crossed his arms over his chest defensively. Kyle didn't get that. "I did. Yeah." Damn, his eyes were hard a flint. Kyle started wondering what the hell he had done to make the guy so angry at him.

"Well, I just wanted to thank you. You saved my life, and I really appreciate it." He had this whole little speech planned. "I know it's what you do, but I wanted to try to find you and thank you personally." God, the "go away" vibes rolled off this guy in waves.

"Well, I'm glad you're okay." He turned back toward the door and reached for it. Either this was the most modest man on earth and he just wanted to get away, or…. Kyle didn't understand.

"Thanks," Kyle said, figuring he'd done what he'd come here to do and that was it. He stepped toward the door to leave.

"You don't remember me, do you?" Hayden asked.

Kyle looked at him again, tilting his head to the side as he tried to recall where he might have seen him before. He racked his brain trying to place the guy and couldn't. And it wasn't like this man was someone he'd easily forget. He was strong, but not in a bulky way. More like firm and well built with intense eyes and short jet-black hair. But it was the short, sexy hair that caught Kyle's attention most of all. It was perfect and sexy as all hell. No, Kyle wasn't likely to forget walking-sex-on-a-stick Hayden... not in this lifetime, anyway.

"I'm sorry. Should I? Have we met before?" He hated when he was supposed to remember someone and didn't. It made him feel stupid. Although if Kyle made a list of things that made him feel that way, he'd be at it all day. He wasn't the smartest guy in the world, but he hated feeling stupid more than just about anything.

Hayden stepped forward. "Maybe it would jog your memory if you tried to push me into a locker or sent my books sliding down the wet high school hallway." The snarl was menacing, but Kyle barely heard it. He looked into Hayden's steely gaze and felt his own widen.

"My God. I remember you now." He gasped and then groaned before coughing. He pulled a tissue out of his pocket to cover his mouth, concentrated on breathing evenly, and eventually the spasm passed.

It looked like Hayden was about to leave, and Kyle knew he had to say something. Memories of how he had acted back then flooded through him, and Kyle wanted to disappear. There were times when he looked back and wondered what the hell he had been thinking. Somehow, he had thought that tearing down guys smaller than him would make him look bigger and stronger. "God, I was such a dick back then." It was all he could think of to say. It was the truth, but massively understated.

"Huh?" Hayden asked, his arms uncrossing.

"I was such a jerk to you… and to other people." There had been a lot of water under the bridge since then, and a hell of a lot had changed. "And here you're the person who saved my life." He was more than a little blown away by that. "Why would you do that after… well… everything?"

Hayden seemed shocked. "I'm a professional, and that's what I do. I don't get to decide who lives or dies, and I don't let people burn up in a fiery building because I don't like them." The set of his jaw told Kyle that he'd insulted Hayden. Maybe it was best if he simply kept his mouth shut and went on his way.

"I'm sorry for taking up your time." Kyle might as well get out of here with some piece of his dignity intact. He'd come here to thank the person who'd saved him, and he'd done that. "And once again, thank you for what you did—for whatever reason you did it." He pulled open the door and stepped out into the fresh air, breathing deeply just to try to clear his head. Of course he took in too much air and ended up coughing, only this time it didn't seem to want to stop. His eyes watered and his chest ached, and he bent over, willing the fit to end. He tried all of the things they showed him in the hospital, but nothing worked.

"Just relax." The voice was rich, and Kyle knew immediately it was Hayden. "Breathe slowly, in and out. Don't fight it. That's it." The coughing subsided, but Kyle remained bent over, breathing shallowly. "How much smoke did you get?"

"The doctor said I was lucky I was alive. Apparently there was a lot of bad stuff in that fire, and it really hurt my lungs." Kyle straightened up. "Thanks for your help… again." He moved away. "I'll be going now. I won't darken your doorstep again." He headed to his work truck and got inside, then pulled the door closed. He breathed evenly before getting ready to leave.

He couldn't blame Hayden for not wanting anything to do with him. Back in high school, Kyle had been vicious with anyone who was different. It didn't take a shrink for him to understand why he had acted that way. If he was mean and singled out anyone who might not fit the mold, then no one would think *he* was different. Looking back on it, he knew he'd been a coward, afraid of who he was and what he wanted. Hayden had been an easy target. It had been pretty obvious back then by the way he acted and the things he liked that Hayden had fit into the easiest category of kid to pick on. The gay one, the sissy, the kid who would always be on the outside looking in. In other words, the one just like Kyle. But Hayden had been braver and stronger than anyone had given him credit for, and in the end, he'd saved Kyle's life, and now Kyle was the one on the outside, wishing he could figure out where the hell he fit in… anywhere.

CHAPTER 3

"LET ME get this straight," Rachel said as she settled in Hayden's favorite chair. He loved it and had looked all over the area for that one chair that felt just right. Maybe he should have gotten two, but there wasn't room in his small two-bedroom place above the antique store downtown. "Kyle Wilson came all the way out to the station to thank you for helping him, and you basically thumbed your nose at him. Did I miss anything?"

Hayden blinked at her. "I figured you'd understand. You know how he treated me… and you. Remember his little stunt in the lunchroom?" He certainly hadn't forgotten.

"Of course I do. But that was high school, and yes, the man was a douche, but that doesn't mean he is now. You remember when I was volunteering for the children's program at the library? He came in and was so good to the kids, and to me. Let me ask you." She leaned forward in the chair, sipping the martini she'd made herself because apparently Hayden couldn't mix a decent drink on his own. "Would the Kyle we knew in high school have ever stopped by to thank you for anything? Even if you had stopped him from choking on the terrible cafeteria hamburgers, say?" She cocked her perfectly groomed eyebrow at him. Rachel had model good looks. She was stunning and always looked perfect every time she stepped out of the house. She and her wife were the same-sex power couple in town. Claire was a lawyer and currently running unopposed for one of the borough council seats.

Hayden hated that she was right. "So? That doesn't change anything. He made my last three years of high school a living hell. I left fucking town because of him and only came back because of the job. What am I supposed to do? Tell him 'You're welcome and I'm glad I saved the life of the world's biggest asshole'?"

Rachel sighed. "Dude, you can be a real ass sometimes. What I want you to do is leave high school behind. You're an adult, and so is he. Besides, you have what you always wanted, remember? You wanted to be a firefighter in the tenth grade. It was your dream, and you're living it. Kyle is trying to hold together a business as a contractor, but he was working in the house that burned down, so half the town is going to think it was his fault, even if it isn't. He isn't going to be able to work because of the injury, so future jobs are going to be tough." She sipped from her glass. "Oh, and here's the best part. Kyle came out of the closet a few years ago, and his family hasn't talked to him since."

Hayden nearly dropped his glass. "No fucking way."

"Uh-huh. Why do you think his idiot brother doesn't see him? Why do you think the guy is trying to make it on his own? You know Daddy Warbucks Wilson has more money than God, and yet Kyle is struggling. Why do you think Jason can afford to be as big an ass as he is? The guy doesn't need to work, so who cares if he loses his job?" She settled back in the chair, and Hayden knew she had a lot more she could share, but she'd suddenly clammed up. Maybe if he got a few more drinks in her, she'd spill, but Hayden didn't want her repeating any pillow talk. There was no way he wanted either her or Claire to get in trouble.

"And this changes things because…?"

"Knock it off. He was good enough to say thank you, and you should have been big enough to be kind and accept it." Rachel was on one of her crusades, and all Hayden could do was weather the storm. He didn't see where he had done anything wrong. He hated the guy. Why should he have to be nice to him?

"He did have a coughing fit in the parking lot, and I went out to help him. That has to count for something." He was getting tired of this whole conversation and really wanted to change the topic.

"Please." Rachel rolled her eyes dramatically. "You did that out of professionalism, pure and simple." She finished her drink and set the glass on the side table. "I'm just saying that this isn't high school. You're all grown-up now, and so is he. Things change, baby-cakes, and you need to change along with them."

"Fine. If I run into the guy again, I'll try to let the past stay there." Not that he had any intention of seeing Kyle again for as long as he lived. "Why is this such a big deal to you?"

Rachel smiled. "Because hate gives you lines, and honey, none of us are getting any younger. And let's face it, you need to get yourself a man. Find someone to bump uglies with, because you, my friend, are turning into a grumpy old man at the ripe age of twenty-eight."

Hayden did have to agree that she had a point. "Do you remember that one guy I dated, Darren?"

Rachel waved her hand at him. "He doesn't count. The man lived with his mother, and she did his laundry. He was still like a teenager and needed to grow the hell up. When you got serious, he asked you to move in with him… at his mom's. That's just creepy, and you did the right thing running for the hills. Besides, we all knew he was terrible for you."

Hayden sipped his beer. "Then why didn't you say something?" Everyone in his life had opinions, and the one time they kept quiet, he gave his heart to a guy with a severe attachment to his mother.

"Because you had to figure it out for yourself." Sometimes it got under his skin how she had an answer for everything. "Anyway, this is different. Find someone you can spend time with, talk to, and have fun with." Rachel was all about pairing up the entire world now that she had Claire and had settled into domestic bliss. Hayden expected her to announce that she and Claire were going to try to have a kid at any moment. Those two were so blissfully happy it gave him a toothache. He was happy for her, but he just didn't see that happening for him, maybe because he wished it would.

"Why do I get the feeling you're working yourself into something?" Rachel had that look in her eye that sent a chill up his back.

"Claire and I are having a party in two weeks, and we expect you to be there. The county board is gearing up for a fight about a nondiscrimination bill, and we're going to need funds to help get it passed. We're holding a fundraiser so we can support those who will help get it pushed through, and you're coming." This must have been what she had been working toward.

"You know how I am with these things," Hayden said.

"I know. But it's important for people to know that gay people are everywhere—including the hero who just saved a man from a burning building." She grinned.

Hayden should have known she had an ulterior motive. "I'll be there as long as I'm not on shift." There was no use fighting it. She'd get him to agree and then pick out his clothes for him if he put up too much of a fight. Besides, Rachel was his oldest friend. He could be social for a few hours if it meant so much to her. It wouldn't kill him.

"You really want me to dress up for this?" Hayden asked as Rachel pulled his suit out of his closet on the day of the fundraiser.

"Yes, and God, this thing is horrible." She tossed the one nice suit he had on the bed. "There is no way this is going to do." She left the room and came back with a black garment bag with a wide hanger sticking out the top. "I knew you'd need something." She handed him the bag.

"How do you know it will fit?" Hayden asked with a glare.

"Please. I took one of your shirts, and I know that old thing fits because you wore it to that funeral two months ago. I used that as a base and got you something new." She lowered the zipper on a dove-gray suit that even Hayden had to admit was pretty nice. "Go put it on, and wear this shirt. I got a lovely tie to work with it, so you should look amazing tonight." She shooed him off to the bathroom, and Hayden reluctantly put on the suit.

By some miracle it fit, and it didn't pull at the arms when he moved. "It fits well."

"Great." She was already heading to the door. "I've got things to get ready, and Claire is about to kill our next-door neighbor. Apparently he decided to turn on his sprinklers, and they went nuts and sprayed water everywhere. I need to get home, but you come on over at six." She was out the door almost before Hayden could say goodbye and thank her for the suit.

He had two hours before he needed to be there, and more than anything, he hoped for a major fire that the chief would need to call him in for. Hayden hated this kind of thing. Attending one always made him feel like a wallflower. He never knew what to say to people he didn't know. "Oh, just get over it," he told himself. There was no way he was going to disappoint Rachel. He could stay for an hour, eat some food, make a donation, and then disappear and come back home. It was that simple… or at least he hoped so.

"HAYDEN," CLAIRE said as she opened the door. He handed her the bottle of wine he'd brought and hugged her. "I was about to send out a search party."

"I'm only five minutes late," he told her.

"I'm teasing. Come on in. We already have a full house." She ushered him inside and quickly made introductions. Then she breezed off, and Hayden was on his own. He said hello to a few people near him and did his best to join in the conversation, but home renovation wasn't his thing, and he ended up just listening before the group drifted off.

"Honey," Rachel said as she tugged him over to another group. "Everyone, this is Hayden. He's a firefighter, and he rescued the man from that house fire on Pomfret. A real-life hero."

"Geez, Rachel, don't lay it on so thick," he told her as the others chuckled. "I was doing my job. I've done it a number of times." He really didn't want to make a big deal.

"He really did save my life." Hayden knew that voice. He turned as Kyle joined their group.

"Like I said. It's what I do, and I'm always grateful when I can help someone." Could he sound any more like one of those athletes reciting a rehearsed line when a reporter shoved a mic in their face? "Are you feeling better?"

"Were you hurt?" a man in a bright purple shirt that matched his hair asked.

"I got too much smoke, and it messed with my lungs," Kyle answered, and Hayden found himself watching him closely. There was something in his eyes that was so different from Hayden's high school tormentor. Not that Hayden was going to let that get to him. "It's taken a while, but they're getting better, and I'm going to be able to go back to work next week. But it's because of Hayden that I have something to go back to."

Hayden found himself standing a little taller under the praise, even though he had no idea why Kyle was here and why Rachel hadn't told him he would be at the party. "Like I said, I was just doing my job."

"Were you two in high school with me?" the man with the purple hair asked. "Trevor Jackson."

Hayden shook his hand. "We were in English and Spanish together," Hayden said, purposely not mentioning that Kyle had been in that same English class and had gone after both of them. He was at Rachel's party, and he wasn't going to make a scene. However, it was clear that Trevor remembered Kyle as well.

"God, I am so glad those days are over," Trevor commented, and Hayden found himself nodding. What surprised him was that Kyle was doing the same.

"I never want to go back there," Kyle said. "Those years were hard. I thought I knew everything, and now I realize I didn't know crap about what was really important. You and Hayden had a huge head start in that department."

"How so?" Hayden challenged.

"You guys knew who you were and you were willing to just be yourselves." That moment of honesty hit home for Hayden. He had been the person he was.

"And we paid a price for that," Trevor said. "But in the end, I went on to college, and now I administer a statewide charity that fights gay youth homelessness. Hayden here became a firefighter and saves lives… your life, as a matter of fact." That was definitely a dig, and Kyle flinched but didn't say anything about it.

"I have a construction company, and…." Kyle paused and seemed to be searching for something. "And I know that if I had been as true to myself back then as you guys were, that I'd have been one of those homeless kids you help." Kyle backed away, and as Claire circulated, Kyle shifted into her conversation and out of the group. Hayden watched him go, pondering that what Rachel had told him seemed to be true.

"I never would have guessed that," Trevor said softly.

Hayden glanced at where Kyle was talking with Claire and a few of her friends, trying not to admire the way his legs and ass filled out those damned black dress pants.

"I never would have thought he'd have had anything but an easy life. His dad was always there to bail him out." Trevor seemed to have some of the same residual issues with Kyle that Hayden did.

"Things change for all of us," Hayden said.

Trevor smirked. "You certainly have. I remember you being tall but skinny." The way Trevor looked at him—like Hayden was a buffet to be devoured—made Hayden self-conscious. He had spent a lot of time in the gym building up his body in an attempt to wipe away the insecure weakling he'd been in high school. "You're anything but that now."

Hayden's cheeks heated, and he didn't know what to say. Trevor seemed to be coming on to him. He was sure Trevor was a nice person, but that sort of behavior didn't work for him. One of the last guys he'd dated acted that same way. Peter had pursued him hard, and they went out for a few months, but things ended badly when Hayden figured out that to the successful lawyer, Hayden was just eye candy. At least that was what Hayden overheard him saying to a group of guys at a work party. To him, talking that way was just another means of bullying, and he wasn't going to take it.

He knew he had to say something, especially with the way Trevor looked at him like he was dinner. "Thanks. I have to keep fit for my job." Rachel passed close, and he caught her eye. Thankfully she joined him, slipping an arm in his. "Having a good time?" he asked her.

"I am. Thanks." He'd hoped she'd rescue him. "Oh, Trevor, there's a couple in the living room who wanted to talk to you. They support a lot of causes, and I thought they might be people you can work with."

Trevor was off like a shot, and Hayden sighed. "Thanks."

"No problem. You had that deer-in-headlights look." She released his arm. "Did you and Kyle talk a little?"

"What is it with you and him?" he pressed.

Rachel rolled her eyes in that way she had. "High school is over, and I've crossed paths with him a few times. He's not the man he was then. Trevor, on the other hand, isn't either. It seems he's turned into a gvetch or something. If he isn't trying to get donations for his cause, he's trying to get into everyone's pants." She sighed.

"Is that a thing?"

Rachel shrugged. "I don't know. I just made it up." She guided him over to where Kyle stood next to the bar with a glass in his hand.

"When did you turn into such a pushy broad?" Hayden whispered.

"About the same time you turned into a wallflower," she countered. Hayden had always been a wallflower, so maybe Rachel had always been this pushy. Hell, as much as he could complain about it, the truth was he adored her outgoing nature. The bad thing was that she knew it too. "Just play nice and help us out. Everyone is here because they support the ordinance and gay rights. Talk about that." She hip-checked him lightly. "The guy is out, gay, and he's come a long way." She leaned closer. "Besides, he's gorgeous, and he's been through a hell of a lot."

"Are you playing matchmaker? Because, sister, if you are, you're barking up the wrong damned tree."

Rachel laughed softly. "Good God, no. That's a recipe for disaster. Just let go of the old hate, and maybe then you won't have to carry all that shit around with you." She leaned closer. "Besides, you saved his life. That puts you in the relationship driver's seat."

Now it was Hayden's turn to roll his eyes. "Are we ever in the relationship driver's seat?" He glared, and even Rachel had to admit that when it came to Claire, she was putty in her hands. "So give it up."

"Fine. Just talk to the guy," she coaxed, and he took the beer Rachel offered before going over to Kyle.

"I don't usually stay very long at these things," Hayden said as a way to start a conversation.

"Why not?" Kyle asked. "Is it the glittering people all trying to see what they can get out of everyone else?"

Hayden lowered his gaze. "No. I just have never been really comfortable at parties and things. Lots of people drinking, and when they have too much, folks get dumb. When they do that, well… that's when they call people like me to try to get them out of trouble." He sipped his second and last beer of the evening. Hayden never had more than two and probably wouldn't finish this one. It was just something to hold.

"I suppose. I don't really know a lot of these people. Rachel asked me to come. I worked with Claire a few years ago. She bought this house before she and Rachel got together, and I did the kitchen remodel for her."

Hayden smiled. "This is your work?" He was impressed. The space was gorgeous, well planned, and the workmanship was amazing. "It's really beautiful."

"I'm just the builder. Claire has really good taste. But it was my idea to leave the tops of the cabinets open to the ceiling. I added the crown molding, but also a shelf just out of the line of sight. The areas can be used for display without the items needing to be propped up." Kyle smiled slightly. "I love what I do."

"And you seem really good at it. Do you have a lot of people who work for you?"

Kyle shook his head. "I have some subcontractors that I trust, but I pretty much do the work myself. I like to know the workmanship that I'm getting. It takes longer to get the jobs done, but the homeowner gets real quality." He was clearly proud of the work he did.

"Was that what you always wanted to do?" Hayden asked, figuring it wasn't going to hurt him to talk, even though part of him just wanted to get the hell away.

"I was always good with my hands. I wanted to make furniture and things like that, but once I knew that I couldn't make a living at it, I went into construction. I do tile, counters, and cabinets, but my favorite part of the job is the finish carpentry. I like putting on the finishing touches. That's when everything comes together and the place really meets the client's vision of what they wanted in the first place." Kyle seemed animated. Hayden followed him through the house, listening as he explained all the work, but he hung back a bit. Part of him still wasn't sure what to expect or why he was even spending time with Kyle. Hayden's gut told him he should run for the hills, but he didn't and had no idea why. Maybe, as Rachel suggested, he was starting to let some of this go.

CHAPTER 4

KYLE WASN'T sure what he was doing. He continued talking, and Hayden seemed interested, though the guy probably should have been completely bored out of his mind. A beeping pulled Kyle out of what he was saying, and Hayden reached into his pocket to check his phone.

"I have to go," he said breathily, his body going rigid. He looked around the room and strode over to say something to Rachel. Kyle wondered if he had somehow said something wrong or if he'd managed to bore Hayden to complete tears. He had been told that when he got going talking about his work, he could rattle on for hours. Then Hayden turned back to him and said, "I think you should probably come with me."

Kyle's throat went dry. "Why?" he asked warily.

Hayden's gaze held him. "Because they found something out of the ordinary at the house that I pulled you out of, and they've asked me to take a look. I'm hoping you can explain where things were before the fire."

Kyle nodded absently and followed Hayden out of the party to his truck. Once they got inside, Hayden drove to Ellen's house, which had been reduced to a hollowed-out shell. "What did they find?"

Hayden sighed softly. "Some of the tests we sent off to the state lab came back. Accelerants were present in the area where we believe the fire started."

It didn't take long for that concept to sink into Kyle's head. "And you think I would do that?" Kyle snapped.

Hayden turned to him. "If I did, you wouldn't be here in the truck with me." Damn, the man had eyes that could blaze as hot as any fire. "I need you to help me. There isn't much left of the area where the fire started."

"There wasn't much in the house, other than my tools. The old owners had cleared their things out, and Ellen hadn't moved in yet." Kyle tried to think about the basement and the back of the house. "I had been working in the kitchen area, but we were waiting for cabinets and things to come in. The old things had been torn out, but some of the appliances were still there because we were trying to see if any of them were worth anything. Ellen said that I could use them if I needed to while I was working, but I only put a few things in the refrigerator when I was going to be there all day." He kept running through everything he'd done that day, just like he had dozens of times. "There's nothing I did that could have caused the fire unless the wiring shorted out, but I doubt it. The electrical systems were inspected before we started any of the other work. I wanted to make sure there were no issues." At least that was one thing he was fairly certain of.

Hayden nodded. "It wasn't electrical." He stopped the truck and opened the door, and Kyle got out as well. The smell of wet, burnt wood hung in the air. The boarded-up front of the house loomed over them as Hayden led the way along the passageway between the buildings to the back. The damage was much more visible there. The addition that had been put on sometime in the fifties was completely gone, reduced to ashes and a small pile of rubble. "Be careful," he said and wandered down the overgrown yard. The remains of bushes, shrubs, and trees filled the space, leaves black and branches bare and charred, rising up toward the night sky. The space could have been used as the set of a cheap horror movie.

"What are we doing out here?" Kyle asked.

Footsteps approached from the back of the yard. "Hayden."

"Dirk," Hayden answered.

"You didn't need to come out here tonight. We could have met tomorrow." He was a huge man, and Kyle stepped back until he smiled. "Who's this?"

"Kyle Wilson, this is Dirk Krause. He's one of Carlisle's lead fire investigators. I was at a party this evening…."

"And you took the first excuse you could to leave," Dirk supplied. "But why bring a guest? Was he your date?"

Hayden coughed, and Kyle smiled to himself. He and Hayden may have begun to forge a peace between them after what Kyle had done in school, but he didn't see them dating, even if Hayden was hot enough to start a fire on his own. "No. Kyle was the man I rescued during the fire. He's also a contractor, and he knows the property well."

"Okay." Dirk sighed. "Look, what's still in place seems reasonably sound. Don't touch anything, but I wanted you to take a look at some things. The fire burned unusually, and that's part of what made me suspicious." They descended the outside concrete stairs to the basement.

"Is that where the fire started?" Kyle asked.

"In the back here. But I think it started on the ground floor and burned through. That's why most of this is intact. Do you remember what was above here? There's nothing left because it burned so hot."

Kyle glanced upward. "I think it was the laundry area. The old machines had been removed, and it was just empty space. It's also toward the back of the house, away from where I was working…." The thought that he had been in the house when the fire was set sent an icy chill down his spine. "That could mean that someone tried to kill me." All they had to do was cut off his means of escape.

Hayden and Dirk exchanged a look, and then Hayden nodded.

"Unfortunately, that's possible. But it could be that someone has it in for the owner of the property and figured this was the easiest way to get even with her." Dirk spoke almost like he was talking about the weather.

"I don't think you're helping here, Dirk," Hayden said before coming closer. "It is possible that someone is trying to get even with you or Ellen, but it's more likely that we've got a firebug on the loose in town.

This isn't the first fire we've had like this. Remember that house out on South Street last year?" Hayden asked Dirk. "I hadn't been with the department all that long. It was one of my first big fires, and it burned really hot, just like this one."

For some reason Kyle and Dirk ended up sharing a look. "How do you remember that?" Dirk seemed impressed. "And now that you mention it, there are similarities. That house was under renovation as well. So that tells us we have a possible pattern. It isn't likely if they are linked that they had the same owner."

Kyle felt his knees begin to weaken. "No, Ellen didn't own that house. It was a couple moving in because the wife had gotten a job teaching at the war college." Kyle knew the moment the implications clicked for both of them. "Yeah, I was the guy remodeling the house for them. They decided in the end to buy a different place, and the shell was sold, gutted, and only the outer walls were reused. Everything on the inside was going to be new." And Kyle had found himself out of a job.

The silent communication between Hayden and Dirk was nearly deafening. "Okay. But that doesn't mean anything either. So both houses were under renovation. That makes them easy targets. They're empty, and often they're easier to get into."

"Maybe. But it was pretty obvious that Kyle was inside the Pomfret house. He was actively working and probably making a lot of noise." Dirk turned to Kyle, and he nodded, unable to actually speak. To him it sounded more and more like he was the one the firebug was after.

"It's either that or the firebug figured Kyle would be able to get out in time." Hayden seemed insistent.

"Firebugs like to watch. They get a real kick out of see-ing their work in action. The fire, it speaks to them. They don't want to kill people. It's about the fire and watching it do its thing."

"And getting it to behave the way they want it to," Dirk said as he knelt on the basement floor, checking the area and then standing up once more. "I don't think we're going to get anything more down here." He head-ed back toward the stairs as a creak sounded from above them. Dirk put his finger to his lips and led the way back to the basement entrance. They climbed up, and Dirk silently closed the door. Kyle stayed with Hayden as Dirk went to one of the openings that had once been a window. "What the hell do you think you're doing?" he snapped. "Get out of here, now!"

There was a squeak, and then two kids raced across the backyard and over the fence. "Damned teenagers," Hayden swore softly.

"They were looking around. Stupid kids were lucky they didn't fall through the hole in the floor," Dirk said, and Kyle tried to get his head around the things he'd learned.

"What do we do now?" Kyle asked. "What if someone is after me or is trying to put me out of busi-ness by burning out my clients?" A million possibilities ran through his mind, and none of them were partic-ularly pleasant. What the hell was he supposed to do if someone was after him? He'd honestly thought the fire at the South Street house had been an accident. He knew he hadn't caused that one either, but now that there had been a second fire, people were going to put things together, and Kyle could see his business drying up fast. Then what the hell was he going to do?

"I think we need to go over the records of the fire on South Street and see what they can tell us. I'm not sure how that was ruled, but we may need to reopen that report." Dirk made some notes on his phone.

"And what do I do?" Kyle felt a cough coming on. "Is someone going to come after me at home?" After his family turned their backs on him, Kyle had worked hard to make his own way. His grandmother, who was the only one to open her arms to him after he'd accepted himself and come out of what had been a very deep closet, had left him some money, and he'd put most of it into buying a small house.

"I wish I had answers for you," Hayden said. They both looked at Dirk, who didn't seem to have any either.

"Great," Kyle whispered.

Dirk led the way back to the cars. "Stay safe and watch things and people around you. Make sure your home is locked, and if I were you, I'd look into cameras and plenty of lighting. Firebugs are very much people of the shadows, at least in my opinion. So often shining a light will make them think twice. Do you live alone?"

"Yeah," Kyle answered. "Why?"

"It would be best if someone else was there." Dirk turned to Hayden. "Didn't you say last week that your landlord was going to be renovating your building?"

"They said I could stay until they were ready to do my apartment," Hayden said with a touch of panic in his voice. Kyle couldn't blame him. Having Hayden stay at his house was bound to be awkward. The two of them had a messy history, and while Hayden didn't seem to openly hate him any longer, Kyle wasn't sure they could ever be friends... even if Hayden happened to be one of the sexiest men Kyle had ever seen.

Kyle sighed inwardly. If he could do things over again, he'd definitely tell his teenage self that hurting Hayden would have repercussions Kyle could never have foreseen. Not to mention the fact that he'd grown into one hell of a man with eyes that could melt butter and a body just made for every kind of sin Kyle's sometimes wicked mind could think of.

"Maybe. But isn't it just putting off the inevitable? You need to be out of your place for a few weeks so they can redo the plumbing, paint, and do flooring work like the rest of the building."

Hayden shook his head. "What is it with you? You know more about this than me."

"Your landlord is a friend of Lee's. He goes into the shop all the time to talk to George, and they gossip worse than little old ladies. Also, Lee has been helping him with some of the work. I know exactly what they have planned for your place, and it's going to be pretty awesome." Dirk clapped Hayden on the shoulder. "Thanks for coming down. And Kyle, I appreciate your insights. You probably don't need to worry. I really think this isn't about you but about opportunity, or a perceived one anyway." He shook hands with each of them before getting into his truck.

"Well, that was less than helpful," Kyle said as he headed toward Hayden's truck. "What the hell do I do now?" He paused outside the passenger door. "I know that I don't have the best record when it comes to you. I did stuff to you that was pretty mean and stupid back in school. But this is my livelihood and my life, and it looks to me like someone is after me. I'm the one thing in common between these two fires."

"I know you didn't have anything to do with the fires," Hayden said. "No matter our history, I like to think I wouldn't be that blind. But regardless of what Dirk was saying, probably to make you feel better, or maybe it's just because Dirk can be an asshole some-times… I have no idea. But I'd be careful if I were you. At least until we have more to go on."

Kyle looked over the bed of the truck. "Look, I'd feel better if I wasn't home alone all the time, and if you need a place to stay… well, I have a guest room and all. And… well, it's the least I can do to try to make up for all that shit in the past." He didn't expect Hayden to take him up on the offer, but he had made it, and he wasn't going to take it back.

"I don't know what my landlords have planned." Those deep blue eyes met his, glistening with reflected light from the streetlights, and Kyle suddenly wished that Hayden would agree just so he could get to watch him, because damn, Hayden was sex personified… at least to him. Kyle was a guy, after all, and he certainly wasn't dead, even if his sex life had been as sparse as trees in the desert.

Kyle wasn't going to push. There was only so much he could do. Not that he blamed Hayden. He was probably the last guy on earth that Hayden wanted to have anything to do with. "I should probably get back to the party before Rachel gets angry with both of us." He got in the truck, and they both sat quietly for the ride back. "I appreciate you believing that I didn't have anything to do with the fire." A lesser person would have tried to pin the fire on him out of spite. One thing that was really coming into focus was the kind of man that Hayden actually was. It only made him feel worse for the way he'd acted.

"I see you two decided to come back," Rachel said as soon as they rejoined the party. She looped an arm around each of them and guided them back to the group of folks still in the living room. "Did you figure out anything?" she asked. "Work things out?" She drew them both closer. "Screw each other's brains out until you're both just a puddle and can let the past stay there?"

Hayden snorted. "You have a wild imagination. Do you really see me as the fuck-it-out kind of person?"

Rachel sighed like the weight of the world rested on her shoulders. A real zinger was coming, and all Kyle had to do was wait for it. "No. But a girl can hope, can't she?" Damn, her leer was stunning. "And imagine it, because just thinking about the two of you together is almost enough to make me take a walk on the straight side... again. But then, the two of you don't swing my way any more than I do yours, but I will say, hot is hot. And that's one thing I know."

Claire strode up. "Do I have anything to worry about?" There was no heat or jealously in her. She and Rachel were as solid a couple as Kyle had ever met. Rachel turned to Claire and kissed her hard enough to raise whoops and hollers from the assembly.

"You can't take them anywhere," Hayden deadpanned. Kyle snickered. Still, it was amazing to know two people who loved each other that much. It left him more than a little jealous.

Rachel left their sides and returned with wine, pressing a glass on each of them. "Go ahead and sit down, talk to people, relax."

"Have you always been this pushy?" Kyle asked.

"Yes," Hayden answered before Rachel could say anything. "And I love her for it. I swear I'd never get out of the house if it wasn't for her." He put an arm around her, giving a light squeeze. "She's also the first and only girl I ever kissed." Rachel glared at Hayden, making Kyle smile, especially when Hayden seemed to realize what he'd said and blushed beet red. "Sorry. We were both fourteen, and I think we were trying to figure stuff out."

Rachel turned to Claire and moved into her embrace. "And it was after that kiss that I started to figure out I liked girls."

Hayden bowed slightly. "Glad I could help with that, because it was the same for me. Well, that I liked guys." Damn, Kyle loved how quick Hayden's wit was. He suspected the two of them could banter back and forth for hours.

"We should probably figure out our plan of attack to get the antidiscrimination ordinance finally passed before we all get too loaded to think clearly," Claire said, calling everyone to attention. "The first thing is to write letters. I have the email address to send things to. This email address is to the county secretary, and I know that if you address the letter to the county commissioners, then they are all forwarded a copy."

"Good. But we need to put on some pressure. There are plenty of conservative places in the county that could put up a fuss, and we need to make some noise if we want to truly be heard this time. It's stalled two previous times, and we need to get it passed. The state will never do anything, so we need to try to protect our part of it." Claire was great at getting the point across quickly.

The group batted around ideas while Kyle listened. This wasn't the kind of thing he was good at. Now, his mother, she could get people organized and was amazing at bringing attention to her causes, but LGBTQ rights was never going to be one of them. Kyle knew that for damned sure.

"Why not gather stories if we can?" Hayden offered. "Good people don't see this as an issue because they don't even know it happens. They aren't aware that people can be fired or that you can refuse to rent to someone who's gay. Most people think that with marriage equality, the fight is over."

"I know people who were refused an apartment," one of the guys said, but Kyle barely heard him, his attention focused on Hayden. There was something that drew Kyle to him. Maybe he just felt guilty for the crap he'd done when they were in school. That had to be it. Sure, Hayden was hot as hell, but there was no way he would ever see Kyle as anything other than his bully. Not that Kyle could blame him, but it was a damned shame and all his fault.

"My wife and I were turned away from a house in Mount Holly." The woman was a small, demure lady who looked like someone's grandmother. Her gentle voice pulled Kyle's attention back to the conversation. "I'd be happy to tell our story." She smiled, and Claire took her hand. "I bet we can get more and put together an article for the paper."

The conversation continued, but Kyle found it difficult to concentrate. They were talking about things he didn't understand very well. His parents certainly would have, and would probably have had ideas, but that wasn't going to help. It saddened him, and he tried not to let that overtake the excited mood in the room, but it was difficult.

Hayden caught his eye, and Kyle forced a smile, but his mind wasn't into all this right now. If he wasn't thinking about his exile from his family, his mind shifted to who might want to hurt him or destroy his business. The sad thing was that line of thought only led back to his father, who had already threatened him on more than one occasion. It sucked to think that someone could hate him so much. Kyle winced and glanced at Hayden out of the corner of his eye.

He had hated Hayden in high school. Kyle could admit that now, at least to himself. He had been so wrapped up in his own inner turmoil that he'd lashed out at everyone around him, especially guys like Kyle, because then no one would suspect him. Well, at least that was the easy answer. It didn't help that his own family had validated his behavior with their attitudes, ones that cut deep all the time, though Kyle hadn't realized it then. He'd only been this pent-up ball of anger.

"Kyle?" Claire's voice cut through his roiling thoughts, and he snapped back to the present.

"Sorry," he said softly. Claire smiled and lifted the bottle. "No, thank you," he answered. If he drank any more, he'd end up on a one-way trip to completely maudlin, and he didn't need that.

Kyle finished the last of his wine and took the glass to the kitchen, where he set it on the counter. He should probably just go on home and go to bed.

He pulled out his phone to check the time and was about to slip it back into his pocket when a text message flashed on the screen. He opened it and read the message as Rachel came in with more glasses. "What's happened?" she asked immediately.

"I need to go. My neighbor messaged that someone is in my backyard." Kyle thanked her and headed out to his truck. He jumped at a tap on the passenger window and was surprised when Hayden peered inside. He lowered the window. "I gotta leave."

"Rachel told me. I'll follow you."

Hayden left immediately, and Kyle raised the window again, then pulled out and headed through town as fast as he dared. His stone-sided house on the south side had been built in the thirties. If Carlisle had a gay-borhood, then this was it. There were four other gay couples less than a block away, including a doctor and his husband, along with their daughter. He pulled into the drive, his lights scanning the front yard.

Hayden pulled to a stop and parked in front of the house. "Go on inside and turn on all the outside lights."

Kyle did as Hayden instructed while he stayed outside.

"There doesn't seem to be anyone out there." Still, Hayden charged across the yard to his garden shed and pulled open the doors. Fortunately, nothing jumped out into the night. Hayden closed the doors, then checked around the back of the house before joining Kyle near the back door.

"Was anyone there?" Kyle asked.

Hayden nodded. "They were. It rained this after-noon, and some of the ground is still wet. From what I can tell, someone was trying to look in through the back windows." Hayden led Kyle around the back and pointed out indentations in some of Kyle's flower beds near the house. Using his phone light, he illuminated the area. "See, there, and right over here."

Kyle felt his legs weaken. "Jesus."

Hayden bent down and sniffed. "It gets worse. I think I smell gasoline."

Kyle put his hand against the building for support. What the hell was going on, and what was he going to do about it?

CHAPTER 5

HAYDEN STOOD, ready to catch Kyle if his legs buckled. "It isn't much." He tried to calm Kyle down.

"But why in the hell would someone be after me?" Kyle asked.

Hayden clamped his lips closed and guided him toward the back door. Once Kyle was inside, he got a shovel from the shed and dug around in the bed to see if he could figure out how much petroleum had been spilled. The scent seemed to be dissipating, so it couldn't have been a lot. Hayden turned the soil and got the hose, then wetted down the area well and stirred it again. The scent was largely gone by the time he was done. Then he joined Kyle inside.

"I turned the soil, and the scent is dissipating. With the soil and the fact that gasoline evaporates pretty quickly, I think it's okay. I'd like to check it out in the daylight and maybe have Dirk take a look too. But there isn't much left."

Kyle nodded. "What if they come back?"

Hayden didn't have any answers. "Leave the outside lights on. That will act as a deterrent." He wished he had something more concrete. He wasn't the police, though there was little they'd do. Heck, Hayden wasn't even sure the fires were actually connected. This could have just been a homeless person wandering through Kyle's yard. What he did understand was Kyle's worry.

"Is that all you have?" Kyle snapped. "Geez, I'm sorry," he added quickly. "But what if someone tries to burn me out of the house?"

Hayden knew the worry in Kyle's eyes. He had seen it plenty of times in the mirror. What surprised him was the way he wished he could take it away. Where had that come from, and when had he started worrying about how Kyle felt? Part of his world had definitely tipped on its axis, and he wished it would stop. He was supposed to hate Kyle for the way he'd treated him in the past, not care about the guy. Yet here he was, at Kyle's house, because he couldn't let him come home alone in case there was a threat. Hayden did a quick mental check of his faculties, just to make sure he wasn't going crazy. "First thing, let's take it easy. Whoever was here is gone, and I doubt they'll come back tonight."

"But what if they're watching?" Kyle asked.

"Then they know you have good neighbors and you have people who will come to your aid. All of which are good things. That only adds to the danger for them. As for burning you out, that's not as easy as it's shown in the movies. But keep vigilant, and you can call me if you see anyone." He gave Kyle his number. "I'd also call the police. But I have to ask if you know anyone who might be after you."

Kyle paled and then shook his head. "I don't know. Yeah, I was a jerk in school, but we were all teenagers, and hopefully I've grown up a lot since then." He sighed. "Do you want some coffee? I can make a pot." He seemed to need something to do.

Hayden agreed, pulled out one of the kitchen chairs, and took a seat in the warmly decorated room. "Are you trying to change the subject?"

"No. I just don't think I have that kind of enemies. I started my company a few years ago, and I try to make sure my clients get a good value for their money. I treat people fairly, and I never cheat them." He got out two mugs and set them on the counter.

"What about your family?"

Kyle nearly knocked one of the mugs onto the floor but righted it just in time. "I suppose you heard about that." He poured coffee and brought the full mugs to the table. "My dad isn't happy with me, and he refuses to speak to me other than to preach about how I'm going to hell. My mother goes along with him and wouldn't say a thing against my dad. I think she's afraid of him, but I don't know that for sure. She never stands up to him to his face, but when he isn't around… that's a different story."

"Okay. What about your brother and sister?"

"They do and think whatever Dad tells them to, especially Jason. He wants to stay on Dad's good side. He's the oldest and the one voted most likely to be an asshole. Bella wheedles her own way, at least some of

the time. But she won't step too far out of line." Kyle
rolled his eyes. "I'd like to think my father is only doing what he thinks is right, but I doubt he cares about
anything like that. He wants to have control over everyone. With him it's how much can he get others to
do what he wants." Kyle's eyes blazed with anger and
hurt. "What kind of parent turns their back on their
kid... for anything?"

Hayden didn't know about that. "Do you think
your dad would do something like this?"

Kyle rolled his eyes. "I doubt it. Dad yells and
threatens, but he's not exactly a man of action. The guy
sits behind a desk all day, getting everyone else to do
what he wants. He eats two sandwiches and fries for
lunch, a big dinner, and gets zero exercise. I doubt he
could run under any circumstances, unless it was toward a hunk of roast beef or a platter of bacon."

"O-kay," Hayden said softly. "So who else in your
life might want to hurt you?" If someone had Kyle in
their sights, there had to be a reason for it.

"How do I know? Maybe I said or did something
to someone. I don't know. Usually I spend a lot of my
days working."

"A supplier, or maybe someone who you beat out
for a job?" Hayden offered. "What about the house on
South Street? If that's the first incident...." He wasn't
even sure of that.

"I don't know. I was called for an estimate, and
they hired me for the job. I don't even know if there
were others in the running. I just answered their call. It
was pretty much the same with Ellen, except I knew her
before the job, but she told me that my estimate came
in under what she was expecting and that I was available pretty quickly. She said she liked that. I often take

smaller jobs that the bigger contractors aren't interested in. I also do a lot of my own work and am willing to do more specialty work. I had a job a few months ago where the owners wanted the molding recreated to fill some ruined gaps in their entrance hall. I put together the pieces in my shop at home and installed what they wanted. It took time in the evenings because it was really fiddly, but they were happy." Kyle sipped from his mug.

Hayden tried to think of anything further to ask. "Where did you work before you started your own business?"

"Shields and Young. I was a carpenter for them, but they always cut corners and did the crappiest job they thought they could get away with. That wasn't what I wanted."

"Could they have a grudge against you?"

Kyle shrugged. "I don't see why they would. They're huge, and I'm small potatoes. They build two or three dozen homes a year, and I work on smaller jobs. Sure, they may miss my skills, but they didn't really use them anyway. I was just a guy that a project manager slotted into a job."

Hayden wondered how anyone could live that way. He sipped some more coffee. "Maybe this has nothing to do with you at all." Even as he said it, his mind went to what he'd found outside the window. Someone had been out there, but why? And what did they want? Things didn't make sense, and there was definitely a lot he didn't know. He wondered if Kyle was glossing over the people who might not like him. After all, Hayden wasn't a huge fan, but he was willing to concede that a lot of that was their history. Kyle seemed like a nice enough guy now. "Let's look at this differently. Let's say that there is someone after you. Who is your most likely suspect?"

Kyle paused. "Maybe my brother. But I doubt he'd ever do anything like this."

Hayden understood that attitude. No one wanted to think that their brother would hurt them or have enough of a grudge to set fire to where they were working. Still, Hayden had seen weirder things, and the guys at the station had shared stories that made that seem like child's play.

"Have you had to let anyone go?" Hayden asked. Kyle paused, his eyes widening slightly. Maybe they were onto something. Hayden leaned forward. "What are you thinking?"

"I had a man working for me. A guy about twenty. He was a general helper sort of person. Fetch and carry, doing basic jobs to save time. Except tools kept coming up missing, as well as supplies. I followed him, and sure enough, he unloaded a bunch of stuff from the work site out of his trunk. I got everything back and fired him. He was angry, but I scared the hell out of him with a threat to call the cops if he made trouble." Kyle drank his coffee. "I did the guy a favor. It could have been a lot worse for him. I was just happy to get my stuff back and to have him off my job site."

"How long was it before the house caught fire?" Hayden asked, wondering if this was the connection.

"Maybe a few weeks, I guess. I didn't really think about it at the time. But I don't think Chuck was in town. I heard that he moved south after I fired him, so I don't even know if he was in the area at all."

Hayden asked for his full name and made a note of it so it could be investigated.

He ran out of questions and sipped the coffee, but mostly he ended up watching Kyle. There was something about the man as he was now that drew his attention, something Hayden knew was a bad idea. He really did need to be a big enough person to let the past go, but that didn't mean he needed to be attracted to the person today. That was a step too far. And yet sitting at Kyle's table, he found himself watching the way his arm muscles bunched as he lifted his mug and how his full lips touched the rim of the cup. The ideas that raced into his head were ones he shouldn't be having. "Look, I should go." He set his empty mug on the table and stood up. "Thanks for the coffee."

"You're welcome," Kyle said softly, biting his lower lip.

Hayden left and went out to his truck. He checked the area around the house in case anyone was lingering before heading to his apartment. He let himself in and found a note on the floor that had been slipped under the door. The landlord wanted to get into the apartment starting on Monday. They wanted to complete the renovations on all the units, and the flooring and appliance people were available that week.

Hayden knew he couldn't really say no. Carrie and George were good landlords, and they wanted to make improvements to make his home nicer. He couldn't complain. Yeah, that meant he needed to find a different place to stay for a while.

Kyle had offered, but Hayden didn't want to take him up on it. Things as far as Kyle was concerned were just too damned unsettling. What he needed to do was just stay away from him and let things settle down. He hadn't seen Kyle in years, and lately he was there every time Hayden turned around. What had to happen was he would go back to his normal life: work, the apartment, quiet, and routine. That was what he liked. Kyle could go back to his, and maybe it would be another five years before they saw each other again. By then maybe he'd be rid of these ideas that kept running through his head—ideas about what Kyle was like under those clothes of his, or what those lips of his would taste like.

Hayden shook his head to rid himself of those notions. He had to be on shift in the morning, and it was already late. What he needed to do was just go to bed, though he doubted he was going to sleep very well… and he was right. The coffee and thoughts of Kyle kept him awake for most of the night.

"HEY, CHIEF," Hayden said before entering his office to relay the details of the evening before. "Dirk is taking the lead, but he asked for my opinion."

"I see." Hayden wondered what that meant. "Why did he take you?"

Hayden shrugged. "Because he and I know each other. He knew I had worked the fire." Hayden took the seat the chief offered. "Dirk had Kyle come along too. He's the guy I rescued."

The chief leaned forward. "And you didn't think that suspicious? He could have set the fire."

Hayden shook his head. "I don't think so. Dirk is checking on the other fire we think might be connected. They didn't think about it at the time, but now he's seeing what the cause of that fire was. We've had suspicious fires before, but…."

The chief nodded. "A firebug isn't something we've dealt with very much. Have Dirk keep you informed, and make sure I'm in the loop. And be careful.

You don't want a target on your back." The chief seemed to be thinking. "I have to ask how you can be so sure that Kyle isn't involved." His gaze was hard and serious.

"I'm not sure." Part of it was a gut feeling. "He and I have a history that isn't good, but I still don't think he's involved. I found him in the front, and the fire started in the back. Why would he let himself be caught in the house and nearly die in a fire he set himself? I think it's more likely that he's the focus of the firebug's ire, but I don't know why yet. It's just a theory."

"I see."

"I know I'm not as experienced as some of the other men, but my gut usually doesn't steer me wrong. And it's possible that there is someone hanging around Kyle's house. Don't know if it's the same guy." This whole situation was filled with questions he didn't have answers for. That alone was unsettling. Hayden liked it when things were wrapped up.

"Too bad we don't have a way to stay close to him. I'd hate for an arsonist to get the entire town on edge. All it will take is a story in the paper or folks to get wind of a serial fire starter and we'll have plenty of pressure on us. The police as well."

Hayden cleared his throat. "My place is being renovated, and Kyle offered to have me stay with him during that period." This was a bad idea. Why had he even told the chief? Sure, he wanted to help, but….

"Then take him up on his offer. Make sure he stays safe, but keep an eye on things. If there is someone hanging around, and if Kyle is the target of a possible arsonist, then maybe you can discover who they are and help us put a stop to this before it gets out of hand. You're going to need a place to crash anyway, and this will kill two birds with one stone." He grew quiet, and Hayden nodded absently. This was a bad idea for a number of reasons that he wasn't going to talk to his chief about.

"I'll talk to Kyle," Hayden agreed. That was as far as he was willing to go right now.

"Good." That seemed to be the end of the conversation.

Hayden left the office to go back to work just as the alarm sounded and everyone scrambled to the trucks. Hayden got into his gear and jumped on. He had never been so grateful for a fire call. At least he would have something to occupy his mind so he wouldn't have to think about Kyle and his damned huge puppy-dog eyes.

"IS THAT offer to stay with you still good?" Hayden asked once they returned from the call, which turned out to be a small grease fire. They had it out in a matter of minutes. Mrs. Kinnear was grateful for the help and offered them brownies she had made earlier in the day.

"Sure," Kyle answered. "What changed?"

"My landlords have asked me to be out sooner than planned." Hayden figured it best not to get his chief involved. "Did anything else happen last night?"

"Other than me jumping at every noise all night long? No." Kyle sounded tired. "Sorry. I'm on edge and have been all day. Of course my offer is open. I have a nice guest room." It was pretty clear that the events of the day before had really gotten to him. "I'm hoping to be able to go back to work soon." He began to cough, and Hayden wished he could help. Damn, he was really starting to like Kyle, which only riled things up even more.

"Take it easy. They want me out in a few days. I won't need to bring a great deal with me. The landlords said that the workers would move the furniture and then put it all back in place when they were done. Let me get back to you with timing after I talk to them."

"Okay," Kyle said softly. "Just let me know. Oh, and tell me the kind of things you like to eat so I can make sure I have some things in the house for you."

"Thanks." Hayden ended the call, wishing on some level that Kyle had been the asshole he remembered. It would make things a hell of a lot easier. But then maybe this was the best outcome after all. Kyle might have been his bully back then, but if he could change enough to be someone that Hayden might actually like, maybe Hayden could be a big enough person to let go of the past. It was hard, but he needed to try. After all, Kyle was actually helping him out when he needed it.

Well, Hayden thought, *time will tell if a leopard can truly change his spots.*

CHAPTER 6

"Are you all right?" Hayden asked as soon as he carried his suitcase in the front door.

Kyle felt like crap and must have looked like it too. He hadn't slept well in days, and every noise, inside or out of the house, had him worried that someone was there, ready to set the house on fire. Dirk had been over to check out the area under the window, but said that other than some form of petroleum, he wasn't sure what it was. Kyle's imagination kept churning over the idea that someone was going to try to burn him out of his house.

"I'm okay," he lied through his teeth. "Come on in."

Kyle showed Hayden down to the guest room and left him alone to unpack. Kyle settled on the sofa, trying to get himself to relax. Hayden was here with him, and that alone made him feel better. If something happened, Hayden would know what to do and who to call for help.

Kyle had never thought of himself as helpless, but over the past few days, he sure as hell felt like it. He kept wondering if someone was outside, stalking him. Of course, he never saw anyone and knew it was probably only his imagination, but still. Sleeping through the night was nearly impossible—when he did manage to doze off, he woke up a dozen times wondering what any little noise was.

"Are you hungry?"

"I am a little. I had a full day, and I was called in early." Hayden flopped down on the sofa. "How did things go here? Are you back to work?"

"I went in for a few hours to clear up some tasks," Kyle said. "Mostly I sit around and try not to cough up a lung. The doctor said I got a pretty bad dose of smoke and that I really need to give my lungs time to heal, but that's hard when there isn't any money coming in unless I can finish something off so I can get paid." He tried to keep his breathing even, but his heart was racing. Kyle had gone over his bank accounts, and he really needed some cash flow. He had enough to get him through a few more weeks, but after that he was going to be hurting. His insurance covered most of the medical expenses, but it didn't help with his loss of income. "I'll be okay. I just have to get better, and fast." He pushed that out of his mind for now. Hayden didn't need to hear him complaining. After all, Kyle was here now because Hayden had rescued him in the first place. "Is pasta okay? I have some sauce that I can heat up and the stuff for salad. I went to the store and got the things you said you liked." Living with someone was going to be strange, but he would do his best to make the time as comfortable as possible for Hayden. Kyle was just grateful to have him here.

"You don't need to watch out for me. I'm pretty used to taking care of myself," Hayden said.

Kyle got up and set down a box of cavatappi on the counter. "I know that. But I was going to make myself some dinner, and it doesn't make sense to just cook for me." He sat down across the breakfast bar from Hayden. "Look, we can either tiptoe around this or just talk about it." Maybe getting things out in the open would be best. "I know I treated you like crap in school, and I feel bad about that. But I'm not that guy anymore." God, he really hoped not. "I know who I am now."

Hayden's posture softened. "I know that. It's just difficult when my initial reaction is to be defensive around you. It's an old habit that I didn't think would still be there, but it seems it is."

Kyle nodded. "Do you think you can get past it? I mean, you're here for a while until they finish your apartment." He figured being honest was the best thing to do. "And I'm glad you are. I haven't slept in the past few days. I'm tired and scared all the time." He looked deeply into Hayden's incredible big, expressive eyes. "I need you." He wanted to reach for Hayden's hand, but he held back.

"That is something I never expected to hear," Hayden said and then smiled brightly. "And yes, I think I can put the past behind us. After all, I'm not the kid I was then. We both grew up."

Kyle nodded, because *damn* had Hayden grown— in so many ways, and all of them seemed sexy. Kyle knew he needed to push those thoughts out of his mind, because while he and Hayden had just agreed to try to be… well, maybe friends… he didn't think Hayden was ready to know that Kyle found him the very definition of hot. That was too far. It was best if Kyle kept that bit of information to himself. Just because they were two gay men and Kyle found Hayden sexy didn't mean that the interest was reciprocated. "Yes, we did. Life has a way of throwing curveballs."

Hayden chuckled. "Sure does. I'm actually here in the same house as you. Now that's a curveball if I ever saw one." He leaned forward a little. "But sometimes those curveballs can turn into some of the best things ever. It's all a matter of timing and figuring out how to make the best of things."

"I suppose you're right," Kyle agreed before getting up. "So are you ready to brave some of my cooking?" He opened the freezer and pulled out a container of red sauce, then popped it into the microwave on the defrost setting.

"Is that a test of bravery?" Hayden asked.

"You'll have to taste it to find out." He liked that they could tease. Maybe they were making progress getting beyond their past.

"THIS IS awesome. Did you make it?" Hayden asked after tasting the sauce. "Really?" he added when Kyle nodded.

"Yeah," he answered. "I like to cook, but I don't do it all that often. I usually work as late as I can to get the jobs done, and cooking for one is never a lot of fun. I make things like sauce and soups, then freeze them to have later. It's either that or eat the same thing for a week." He shuddered at the thought. "Now, please finish making the salad and we can have dinner." Kyle grinned and got out of Hayden's way, because he looked lethal with that knife. "Hey."

Thankfully Hayden stopped. "What?"

Kyle moved behind him. "Use the knife like this." He reached around and showed him how to hold it. "Now use fluid strokes and curl your fingers under slightly. Like that." Kyle waited for Hayden to comply. "Then lift the knife and slide the lettuce under it, and don't move your fingers." He inhaled, and his head went light for a few seconds. "That's it. Move slowly until you get the feel for it."

"Wow. That's easier."

Kyle moved back. "Isn't it? And you're less likely to cut your fingers or put out your eye," he teased.

Hayden groaned but continued using the knife much more carefully. "I wasn't that bad," Hayden protested and then chuckled. "Okay, maybe I was." He added the lettuce to the bowl, followed by sliced cucumbers and the rest of the fixings. Then Kyle pulled out a jar from the refrigerator. "What's that?"

"My ranch dressing. I make it myself." Kyle smiled as Hayden's eyes widened. "Everything tastes better when you take the time to do things yourself." He gave Hayden a taste, and he nodded.

"Can't argue with you there."

Kyle dressed the pasta and got out dishes. Once everything was ready, they ate sitting across from each other at the breakfast bar, and for a second Kyle could imagine this as a sort of first date. Wine, good food, nice company. He even looked Hayden in the eyes, and for a few moments this fantasy wafted around him.

He didn't let it last long. Fantasies were something he had stopped indulging in. He'd grown up with the grand fantasy that his family would love him no matter what, and that had been shattered. Now he tried to live in the real world, based on what was solid, rather than putting his faith in something as ethereal as a dream or his parents' supposed love.

"This is all so wonderful," Hayden said between mouthfuls and soft moans with each bite. When his phone chimed, he picked it up and sent a message before setting it down. "There's a fire call in progress. It doesn't involve me right now, but I could be called in if I'm needed."

"You act like it's no big deal," Kyle said.

"It is, of course. But not all of us can respond to every call. The guys on shift will handle it. If necessary, they'll call in more companies like they did when I rescued you." Hayden took another bite. "Because the building was downtown, Union was the first unit called. We came in to assist them. That's why I was there and why Dirk is heading the investigation into the fire. It was their call."

"Then why the message if they don't need you?"

Hayden shrugged. "Because I'm on call, like a doctor, I guess. We all take some of these kinds of reserve shifts. I have to stay in town is all. It's part of the salary, and it's never a hardship." He took another bite of the pasta, and Kyle followed the fork as it passed his lips. Damn, even the way he ate was sensual, and the way his eyes half closed as he took that initial taste sent the temperature in the room rising enough that there might have been sweat breaking out on Kyle's forehead.

The motion lights in the backyard came on, and Kyle tensed instantly, his attention pulled to the window. He peered out and then went over. He didn't see anyone, but something had triggered the lights.

"It could be a squirrel or something."

"I don't know. It seems to happen every night about this time. At first I thought it was a car or something in the alley beside the yard, but I've seen huge trucks go down after dark and nothing happens. I even walked the yard to see where it triggers, and it isn't until I'm on the property." He sat back down and forced himself to eat the rest of his dinner. After a few minutes, the lights went off again. Kyle was determined not to get himself all worked up.

"Let me check things out after dinner," Hayden offered. "I'll see what's going on."

"Thanks." Kyle was getting jumpy. "I'm trying not to feel unsafe in my own house." He swallowed and steadied his breathing so he didn't go into a coughing jag. He had found out that as long as he stayed calm, he was fine. The doctor had also told him to get breathing equipment for work and to use it regularly. They said that once he went back it would help continue his healing.

"Do you have jobs set up?"

"Some small ones. Why?"

"Well, my landlord usually does a lot of the work himself, but he's getting older. I can ask him if he could use some help. That would get me out of your hair faster, and it could get you some work at the same time."

"At this point, I'd appreciate anything I can get." Work was good, especially the kind that was somewhat flexible.

Hayden pulled out his phone and sent a text message. A few minutes later, his phone dinged with a response.

"I got an answer from George. His wife says he needs help." Hayden laughed. "So you're in. I'll text you his number. George is a great guy, and he loves his projects. He can't do what he used to, but he still tries."

"I got it. Work with George and help him."

Hayden nodded. "Thanks. I really like him and his wife. They helped me a lot when I was first trying to get out on my own. If I had a problem, he always came right away and fixed it. He's a really good person, but he had a health scare about six months ago. I don't know what it was, but he's slowed down a lot."

Kyle understood. "I learned a lot of what I know from my grandpa. He used to have this great workshop in his basement, and we would make things together. Some of my hand tools are the ones he used to have." He finished his pasta and salad and took his dishes to the sink. As he turned to sit back down, the backyard lights came on again, and he hurried to the window.

"Something is definitely going on." He hated that he was this jumpy.

Hayden took his things to the sink. "Let me look into it." He went out through the back, and Kyle finished cleaning up.

But a moment later Hayden hurried back inside, pushing the back door closed behind him. "I didn't see anything, but I have to go in to work." He grabbed his keys and raced back toward the door. "Lock up, and I'll be back as soon as I can." Then he was gone, and Kyle locked the doors and then finished the dishes before settling in front of the television. He kept part of his attention on the window just in case the damned lights came on again.

FOR TWO hours Kyle alternated between looking out the window and wondering if Hayden was okay. He knew Hayden could take care of himself. Hell, he'd saved Kyle's life after all. But…. God, he was turning into his mother. She had always been a worrier, and Kyle used to tease her about it. Now *he* was one, and it was all Hayden's fault. The worst thing was that he had no right to worry. Hayden was a grown man and could damned well take care of himself.

When his phone vibrated on the coffee table, he snatched it up. "Hey, Rachel."

"God, you sound breathless. Did you run to the phone or something?"

"I'm fine," he told her. "What's up?"

"I heard there was a fire at the old carpet factory." She seemed worried. "It's bad."

"Hayden was called in," he told her. "He left a few hours ago. Is it stupid that I'm worried about him?"

Rachel chuckled. "Yeah, kind of. But is it dumb that the guy you picked on all through high school is the one to save your life?" Damn, she could be snarky.

"He and I decided to let the past stay in the past. We talked over dinner, and you were the one who sort of pushed us to bury the hatchet, so no bringing it up."

"Okay, okay." She sounded pleased. "I was calling to see about you doing some bathroom work for Claire and me. I want to update the bathroom rather than re-model it. These old houses are so temperamental, and when you change things, everything gets messed up. So new counters, fixtures, refinish the cabinets maybe, and do something with the floor, that sort of thing."

Kyle wanted to cry. "You're kidding." He found it hard to believe that the people he had been horrible to in high school were the ones coming to his rescue. That was almost more than he could understand. "That's great. I'd love to. But I have to ask something. Did I fall off the end of the earth and into another dimension?"

"No," Rachel said, laughing.

"Then why?" He had to know. It certainly was nothing he had done. He couldn't quite figure it out. "What's the deal? I don't deserve you and Hayden being so nice to me."

Rachel hummed softly. "Did it ever occur to you that Hayden and I were always this nice? If you had been friendly to us in school, you would have known that then. We'd have circled the wagons around you in order to protect who you were. That's what we did for each other, and we're doing that now. I know why you acted like you did and that when you came out, you paid a high price."

Kyle wandered through the house, glancing out into the dark yard as he talked. "I know. But that doesn't explain why you're being good to me like this."

"Okay." Rachel was silent, and for a second Kyle thought he might have lost the connection. "I think you're a good person. I could see it in high school. You may not remember it, but there was that stupid senior bus trip to Philadelphia. Do you remember?"

"Yes," Kyle said tentatively. "At least parts of it. We snuck on a thermos of punch that had been laced with vodka, and I got pretty plastered." He had never admitted that to anyone. "So there are parts of the trip that are pretty spotty."

"I know. You were drunk and sitting in back with your friends. You know, the assholes. And they were being really mean to Hayden. In fact, they made that trip pure hell for him, right up until you got up and smacked one of them on the side of the head. You could barely stay standing, but you got him to stop, and then I remember the moment you met Hayden's gaze. I saw in that moment what was really going on."

"And what was that?" Kyle challenged.

"That maybe you weren't the asshole I thought you were. That maybe you were putting on an act of some kind. You were drunk, but instead of being a bigger ass, you actually stood up for Hayden." Kyle didn't remember that at all, though maybe what Rachel said was the truth. He recalled parts of that trip, but mostly he'd been miserable and wanted to get outside himself by any means possible, and alcohol was as good a way as any.

"I hated who I was back then," he said softly. "I didn't want anyone to know, and yet I had these intense fantasies about other guys—something I knew I could never have. And then there was Hayden, who was out and didn't seem to care what anyone thought, and I went after him because he could have what I couldn't. I know it's no excuse now, but...." He'd had plenty of time to think about all of that over the past week.

"I guessed at something like that," Rachel said. "And remember that we were on the outside looking in, Hayden and me. I saw a lot of things others didn't realize. I watched you help one of the other kids in gym class on one of those days when boys and girls were together. It was like you'd forget the role and just be yourself for a time. That was when the real you came through." Damn, she really had been watching him.

"Did you like me back then?" Kyle asked.

Rachel snorted. "Not that way. I always liked girls. But you were kind of fascinating to me. See, once I figured out it was all an act, it was easy to see through it. Hayden had no idea, but I did." He could almost see her smiling. "And for the record, I'm sorry about what your parents did to you. That really sucks."

Kyle shrugged as the lights flashed on in the backyard. He glanced outside in time to see Hayden enter through the back gate. He breathed a little sigh of relief that he was back. "Thanks. But they are what they are. I had to accept who I was, and that my family would think how they did and act however they wanted. I can't change that any more than I can alter the fact that I think Hayden is smoking hot." Had he just said that without thinking—and to Rachel of all people? "It is the way it is." He figured it was best if he just went on.

Of course Rachel gasped. "You like him?"

"I didn't mean to say that, and you cannot say anything. He and I just formed a truce, and he isn't going to appreciate anything like that from me. So just forget it, okay?"

Rachel snickered. "Is this some hero worship sort of thing?"

"No. It's an 'I should have kept my mouth shut' sort of thing, and you need to forget I said anything at all. Got it?" he added, a hint of snap in his voice. Like that would work. Rachel was like a dog with a bone when it came to good gossip.

"Kyle...." Rachel had this deep, throaty voice thing going on. "What's going on?"

"I don't know," he answered, his insides in knots. He felt like he was on the verge of coming out of the closet again, but this was so much bigger than that, like the secret he never even let himself acknowledge. "Just drop it, and you forget all about what I said earlier. I'll pay you in chocolate."

"Fine. I won't say anything." She made the promise sound like medieval torture of some kind.

"Good. I gotta go. Hayden is back." The touch of excitement that ran up his spine almost made him angry. He should not be allowing himself to feel this way. It was a recipe for complete disaster. He hung up and went to the window. Hayden made a circle of the yard and came back inside. "Everything okay?"

Hayden yawned and nodded. "We got the fire out, but it was touch and go. There are still a few old industrial relics in town, and this was one of them. We weren't sure what was stored in the building. The chief was afraid we'd have to evacuate the north half of town if we didn't get the blaze under control." He took off his outer layer of smoky clothes, brought it to the garage, and returned. Hayden's sweat-soaked T-shirt hugged his chest enough that the outline of his nipples was visible through the fabric… and what a chest it was. Kyle forced his gaze elsewhere, which only led to further trouble with the way his boxer briefs hugged his hips. Damn, that was a hard sight to look away from.

"But everyone was okay?" Kyle got a bottle of water from the refrigerator and pressed it into Hayden's hand.

Hayden drank without seeming to think about it, downing half the bottle in one go. "Yeah." He set the bottle on the counter. "God, that felt good." He inhaled deeply, his chest heaving with each breath. In Kyle's increasingly feverish imagination, some of that was for him—but of course it wasn't… and it shouldn't be. All this attraction was wishful thinking on the part of his long-denied brain, and it needed to stop. "Everyone is okay." He drank some more and turned away.

"I saw you walking the yard." Kyle needed to get his mind off Hayden.

"I didn't find anything. The lights came on when I thought they should, and I didn't see any footprints or anything. I think it's probably some animals scurrying through the yard and triggering the lights. I also checked with Dirk about what was under the window, and he said he thought it might have been someone

dumping something. It was right behind the house."
Hayden shrugged, and Kyle let himself feel better.

"Okay. So… maybe someone isn't trying to kill
me?" He couldn't figure out who might hate him that
much.

"I don't know. Maybe we're seeing things that
aren't there. Dirk is still looking into the cause of the
original fire and similarities to the more recent one. I
know you were working on both houses, but that might
be a coincidence. I think it's more likely that if there
is a firebug, he's interested in buildings that are being
worked on. It's often easier to get in and out, since usually no one is there. Most of them aren't interested in
hurting anyone. They want to watch the flames."

Kyle shrugged. "I don't get that."

"Well…." Hayden pulled out one of the stools and
sat down. "I guess the best I can explain it is that as a
firefighter, I'm learning how fire works. It needs fuel
and it needs oxygen. Take away either of those and it
dies. If it has both, then it becomes like a living thing.
It moves and runs, like a stream, taking the path of least
resistance to where there's more fuel. It can jump, and
it can also lie dormant for a time until the conditions are
right and it can run." Hayden spoke almost reverently.
"But the important thing is that it can consume itself.
Once a fire runs out of things to burn, it dies away." He
had this wistful expression that almost left Kyle wondering if Hayden had a fascination for the flames. Maybe it was a "dark side of the Force" sort of thing and a
firebug got seduced to the wrong side.

"Is fire something that fascinates you?" Kyle asked
and wondered if maybe he should have kept quiet.

Hayden's gaze darkened. "It does. But not in the
same way as a firebug. I want to put the fire out because

I see its danger and the way it can hurt. The firebug sees the flame as a thing of beauty. Maybe they want to control it, or maybe they want to see if they can set it free and watch it dance. Who knows? Some people just want to see what they did on the news or the internet. They like the power that it gives them. Others want to watch their handiwork, so they stay close to the fire. Faces in the crowd, things like that." He bit his lower lip. "And then we have the simple arsonist who sets fire to the building so they can collect the insurance or something like that. Those people are in a different category. They have a business or maybe a political aim. The firebug is interested in the fire and the flames."

"Okay. But what do you think we have going on?" Kyle asked. "I know Ellen didn't set the fire to burn herself out."

"No. And the fire seems to have been intentionally set. So I do think there's someone out there who set it. Why, I don't know. And that's the big question, and the one Dirk and I need to answer."

Kyle sat as well, his chair maybe a foot and a half from Hayden's, something Kyle was very aware of. He fixed his gaze on Hayden's knee, moved it up to his beefy thigh, and then to the bulge in his sweat shorts. Then he looked away, remembering he shouldn't be doing that.

"What do you do when you aren't helping people improve their houses?" Hayden asked.

Kyle breathed a sigh of relief. "I used to build furniture, and I have a shop in the basement. Right now I use it mostly to construct pieces for jobs. I don't have a lot of free time to make furniture. In the summer I do yardwork. In the winter I sit around, watch football, and yell at the television."

Hayden laughed. "Me too. I have to ask, are you one of those people who thinks they know better than the refs and the coaches?"

Kyle raised his hands. "Of course. None of them know what they're doing, and the refs are always blind as bats." He grinned. "Yelling at the television is half the fun. Otherwise I'd just end up sitting there." His grin was infectious. "What about you?"

Hayden shrugged. "I'm not very exciting, as my last boyfriend will tell you."

Kyle leaned forward. "Excuse me?"

"It was a while ago. Steven liked to go out and had a huge group of friends. Every weekend he had some social function and kept trying to drag me along with him. Sometimes I had to work, and other times I was just tired. It's not like we sit around the station waiting for a fire. We're busy all the time, and it isn't just fires that we respond to. If there's an emergency, we're the first ones called out. It takes a lot of effort to keep all the equipment in top condition. Our lives, and those of the people we help, depend on it." He was so serious. "Anyway… sorry for getting on my soapbox. Steven said he understood at first, but then he started getting angry. Finally he accused me of loving my job more than him, and he told me that I had to be the most boring man on earth and that he was going to find someone more fun. The last time I saw him, he was with a hipster all dressed in black, with more makeup than a drag queen, on his way to some big party in Harrisburg." Hayden nodded. "At least he seemed happy."

Kyle rolled his eyes. "Are you always like that? You look at the bright side of everything."

"What am I going to do—complain and whine all day? That doesn't get me anywhere, and in part he was right. I am kind of boring. I work a lot and spend a good share of my spare time working out to stay strong and fit, and just... I don't know... living my quiet life." Hayden shrugged it off, and Kyle liked that. "Besides, he did me a favor. I really think we would have driven each other crazy.

"Why's that?" Kyle asked. "Was he a bad guy?" He was definitely stupid if he let Hayden go. Kyle had realized just how badly he had messed up all those years ago. Because he had been an ass in school, he could very well lose out on one of the best men he'd ever met.

"No. Just different from me. He wanted to go out and have a good time. I was already training to be a firefighter, and I had more serious things in my life. The breakup didn't upset me, just the mean way he went about it."

A flash outside the window caught Kyle's attention. He watched as it happened again, then reached for his phone and pulled up the radar app. "I guess we're in for some rough weather." He showed the screen to Hayden, who slipped off the stool and hurried outside. Kyle stood as well and went through the house to close the windows.

"I checked everything outside, and it's all battened down. The wind is coming up." A roll of thunder cut him off, and Kyle checked the radar again. The line of storms was nearly on them. "I have my gear in my trunk. I pulled it under the overhang, and I have a clear shot out in case I have to go again."

"Do you get a lot of fires because of lightning?" Kyle asked.

"Not usually. It's the wind. There are so many old trees in town that limbs come down." Another crack of thunder split the night, and then everything plunged into darkness, the only light coming from the next streak of lightning that seared outside the window, followed by the wail of tornado sirens. Kyle knew that wasn't good.

CHAPTER 7

"LET'S GET to the basement," Hayden commanded.

Feeling his way along, Kyle carefully led the way to the door before remembering to use the flashlight on his phone. They descended the stairs, and Hayden followed, hoping he didn't fall and break a leg.

Hayden's ears felt like they were going to pop as they reached the bottom of the stairs. A light flashed on, and Kyle pressed a flashlight into his hand. At least he could save his battery.

The storm outside intensified as thunder and lightning followed each other in rapid succession. He could still hear the warning sirens.

"Let's get away from any windows." He grabbed Kyle's hand to pull him into the laundry area. "This isn't going to last long. These things generally pass quickly." A lot of the time the sirens were only a precaution. It was better to warn people just in case than to miss something that could be dangerous. Hayden stood near the washer, listening for the telltale deep rumble.

"Why aren't you scared as hell?" Kyle's voice broke.

The truth was that Hayden was petrified. He hated storms like this. But he had been trained as a first responder, and the fact that fear could cost him his life had been drilled into him. He had to remain in control and think clearly so he could get out and save lives.

"Because I need to stay alert." He checked his phone, hoping he didn't get called back in. His phone stayed silent. He still had a signal, which meant the towers hadn't gone out. But the storm raged outside.

After ten tense minutes where they talked about nothing just to try to stay calm, the sirens quieted, and Hayden guided them back upstairs. It was still raining heavily, but the wind seemed to have died down, and now it was just a downpour. Hayden checked out the front as well as the back and saw that Kyle had been spared any falling tree limbs. All they could do now was wait for the storm to pass and the power to come back on.

"Is there anything more we should do?" Kyle asked in a soft voice.

"Not really anything *to* do." He checked his phone again. The storms had moved past, leaving behind a front of rain that would probably last for a few hours,

which was going to hamper the efforts to restore power.
Part of him wanted to just go to bed. He was tired. But
he had to stay awake in case he was needed.

Kyle went into the kitchen and flipped on the gas
stove, then put on a kettle of water.

"What are you doing?"

"Making coffee."

Hayden shrugged. It gave Kyle something to do.
Soon enough he brought over a couple of mugs. Instant
coffee wasn't all that great, but it was hot and contained
a jolt of caffeine, which was what he needed.

"Thank you," Hayden said softly as Kyle settled
on the other end of the sofa. He sipped and grew quiet,
letting his racing heart settle to a more normal pace. "I
hate storms," he confessed. "Always have. One tore the
roof off our house when I was about ten. Scared me half
to death, and I've never been able to stand them since."
He sipped some more of the awful coffee.

His phone vibrated, and he checked the message
and answered it to let the station know that he was
okay. Hayden asked if he was needed and received a
message that they had things well in hand. Thankful,
he put his phone aside as fatigue set in. Now that he
didn't have to be on alert, the exertion from the earlier
fire caught up with him. He leaned back, set the mug on
the table, and let himself relax. As soon as he did, two
things became apparent: how tired he was, and how
damned good Kyle smelled.

As soon as the second thought took root, the tired
part of his brain woke back up.

"Do you need to go in?" Kyle asked, his voice
breaking slightly.

"No." He was relieved.

Kyle nodded. "I'm sorry for being jumpy. Maybe I watched too many horror movies when I was a teenager. A group of us used to go to one of my friend's houses, and they always loved slasher movies. The bad stuff always happened on stormy nights like this."

Hayden nodded. "I remember the first one I watched. It was this werewolf movie, and I swear that I was up all night in case they came to try to get me. My mom and dad were so angry with my cousin. She was the babysitter. I was about nine years old." He chuckled softly. "I don't think about that stuff now." He'd seen enough bad things in real life that what might have been on the screen paled in comparison. "I should go to bed." Hayden finished the last of his coffee, took the mug to the kitchen, and placed it in the sink. "I'll see you in the morning." It had been a full day, and he had another one tomorrow.

"Okay." Kyle shifted on the sofa, his legs curled up, arms around his knees. "I'll see you then. Sleep well." He glanced out the window into the darkness but said nothing more.

Still using the flashlight, Hayden turned to go to his room but paused. "Is there something going on? It's just rain. The storm is past, and who knows how long it will be before the power comes on."

Kyle shook his head slowly. "I'm fine here. The lights will all come back on when the power does, so I'll turn everything off." He continued watching out the window.

Hayden remembered that Kyle said he hadn't been sleeping. "Have you been sitting up all night?" He could see Kyle staying up until the wee hours until the fatigue got too much and then falling asleep where he was. Hayden returned to the sofa and sat down, lightly touching Kyle's leg. "You have, haven't you?"

Kyle lowered his head to his knees. "What if someone tries to burn the house down? What am I supposed to do?" His shoulders shook. "The lights in back keep going on all the time. I know someone is out there watching me. They trip the lights just to make sure I know they're there."

"So you think if you stay up all night…." He squeezed Kyle's leg lightly. "We both need to get some rest. I have to get up in the morning, and you need to see George about some work. You can't use tools if you're wiped out." God, what if Kyle hurt himself? "Go on to bed. If anything happens, I'll be here to take care of it. I promise."

He waited, and finally Kyle got up and went to his bedroom. Hayden checked to make sure the house was locked up and went to his room as well. Hayden was too tired to shower, so he brushed his teeth and washed his face, then got ready for bed and slipped under the covers. He spent a few minutes listening in case Kyle got up again, but quickly fell asleep.

He was having the most amazing dream. He and Kyle were teenagers, and they were walking the rail trail by the LeTort Spring Run. They laughed and were having a good time until Kyle kissed him. That made things even better, and they went off into the woods, just the two of them.

Everything grew more heated and passionate. Kyle whispered wonderful things to him. Hayden was going out of his mind, and his teenage self was over the moon. The kissing continued, growing more heated, more passionate. The trees disappeared from around them, and suddenly they were in school and Kyle was still kissing him. No one seemed to notice. Everything was great until Kyle pulled back and pushed him. Hayden stepped away, confused, and then he was falling. Soon cold water covered him.

Hayden woke, confused. He blinked, knowing he'd heard something. He got up and pulled on a T-shirt so he didn't go out in just his underwear. The power must have come on, because the clock by the side of the bed was blinking on and off, telling him little about what time it actually was. He checked his phone, then pulled open the door and stepped out into a quiet house.

Kyle's door was open and the room empty. Hayden softly went downstairs. "Kyle?" he whispered as he went into the living room.

Kyle was on the sofa, the television on a *Golden Girls* rerun. He had fallen asleep and was curled up under a blanket with a large puppy pattern.

"Hey," Hayden said gently.

Kyle stretched and slid his eyes open.

Then he jumped to his feet. "Is the house on fire?" The blanket fell to the floor, leaving Kyle in a pair of red briefs... and nothing else. Hayden didn't answer right away since his mind had skipped a beat. Kyle was lean and strong, with a slight dusting of brown hair in the center of his chest, nice shoulders, and a narrow waist. *Hot* didn't begin to describe him.

"Everything is fine. It stopped raining and the power is back on," Hayden reported.

"Yeah. I turned out the lights about an hour ago. I should probably have gone back up to bed, but...." He seemed to realize how he was dressed and picked up the blanket to cover himself, which was a shame. Kyle presented quite a picture. "Sorry."

Hayden swallowed hard. "Go on up to bed. It's the middle of the night yet, and you need to rest." Hayden waited for him to go upstairs, then followed his now blanket-wrapped form. "Everything is going to be okay." At least he hoped so.

When they were upstairs, Hayden met Kyle's gaze as he turned back. In that moment, he was tempted to push aside his reservations and press Kyle against the wall, maybe his door, or even down onto his bed. The idea sent a wave of desire through him, but he pushed it away. That was a bad idea. His mind knew it loud and clear—but his heart, well, that seemed to be another story. Dammit, he wished the two stupid things would agree on something every once in a while.

THE SCENT of food pulled him out of sleep and drew him downstairs like a siren song. Bacon, smoky and savory, greeted him as he stepped into the kitchen. "I made eggs and toast, and I have bacon in the oven. I can make some sausage if you like." Kyle looked even more tired than he had last night when Hayden had sent him up to bed.

"Bacon is great." Hayden poured a mug of coffee and sat at the table, still half asleep. "That was some storm."

"Yeah. The paper says there were tree limbs down all over town," Kyle said. "I hate weather like that. I did check, and everything here is okay. A few branches came down, but nothing bad." He got plates and set them out, then brought over the toast and eggs before taking the bacon out of the oven. They tucked in.

"What will you do today?" Hayden asked.

"I was going to call your landlord, and I have a few jobs that are close to finished, so I want to try to get them wrapped up. Then I can get my final payment, which should see me through the next month or so." He set down his fork. "I have to figure out a way to bring in some money. Hopefully I can work with George to help him with what he needs." Kyle bit a strip of bacon. "How about you?"

"I'll call the station. I'm supposed to be off today, but they might need me." He sent a message and received a reply from the captain to take the day off, though they would call if he were really needed. He was grateful, because with the number of calls they'd gotten lately, who knew when he was going to get another day. Sometimes things were quiet and the on-call people weren't needed. But lately it had been more and more calls, and that meant Hayden was busy. "It looks like I'm free. I was thinking of checking out some additional security measures around the house here, and I need to call Dirk to see if he's found out anything more. Hopefully I can rest awhile, because I have a long shift tomorrow." Even after last night's sleep, he was still tired. Every time he closed his eyes, he saw Kyle in his dreams, and Hayden wasn't sure that was a good thing.

AFTER MAKING his calls, Hayden settled in for a quiet day. Kyle was off at work, and he had the house to himself. Lying on the sofa, he watched reruns of *Young Sheldon*, just relaxing. His phone beeped and then rang. Hayden knew what that meant. He jumped up, already springing into action before he answered the call.

"I'm on my way." He locked the house, got into his truck, and raced to the station. He arrived in under two minutes, jumped out, and climbed onto the last truck leaving the station.

"House fire," Larson told him as he finished getting into his gear while they moved.

Hayden leaned closer. "Is it under renovation?"

Larson shrugged, but Hayden messaged Dirk to ask what he should be on the lookout for. He got an answer just before they pulled in, and got to work as soon as possible. The building had most likely been derelict. Two of the front windows were boarded up. Hayden grabbed a hose and sprayed water on the nearby structures to keep the fire from spreading.

Movement in one of the other windows caught his eye. "Someone is in there," Hayden called, pointing. He handed off the hose and got into his breathing gear before heading into the building. The inside was filled with smoke, the fire popping in his ears. He didn't see any flames, but that didn't mean they wouldn't make themselves known at any moment.

He checked the front rooms on the lower level. They were empty, with wood and materials stacked off to one side. At least that answered the renovation question. As he headed back, he approached a closed door that radiated heat. Hayden turned away and hurried upstairs, going no farther in that direction.

Hayden was cautious as he went up, knowing it was likely the fire would fan out as he went toward the top of the house. "Anything?" he heard in his ear.

"Not so far," Hayden said. "The fire is hot as hell in the back." He reached the top of the stairs and checked the room directly in front of him. It was empty.

"We have guys on it," he received in response. "Check where you need to and get the hell out," the captain told him.

"I'm on it." He didn't dare go toward the back of the house, so he headed to the area where he'd seen the movement. "Is anyone in there?" Hayden called and opened the door to the front bedroom. He half expected to find someone on the floor the way he'd found Kyle, but instead, two sets of deep brown eyes, wide with panic, stared at him. "I have two dogs up here," Hayden said. He approached the first one, a small wirehaired terrier, who jumped and bounded around his feet. Hayden picked her up, and she squirmed in his arms. He petted her with his gloved hand, and she calmed. The other was a bulldog mix, and he watched Hayden intently. There was no way Hayden was going to be able to carry both dogs. "I've got one, but the other...." He headed to the door. "Come on, boy, let's get out of here."

He carried the little girl out of the room, calling and looking back. At first he didn't think the dog would follow, but then he walked out of the room.

Hayden started down the stairs just as one of the doors blew out. Heat seared behind him, and then the dog raced past him on the stairs and out the front door like the devil himself was on his tail. Hayden didn't waste time either. He got outside and handed the dog off to one of the other firefighters before getting his gear off.

"You saved two this time," Larson teased.

"Hey, I like dogs," Hayden countered. "They're better company than you are, especially with the way you snore." He had worked third shift with Larson when he first joined the company, and no one but Larson slept at all... ever.

"Crap," one of the firefighters called as the little dog jumped out of his arms. It raced over hoses and around other men, straight to Hayden, then jumped and barked around his legs.

"It's okay," Hayden said gently, lifting her into his arms, where she burrowed in as he petted her. "Where's the other one?"

"Danton has him," the chief said. "We're calling animal control to take care of them. The neighbors have seen them around and said they're strays. How they got in the house...."

"Behind a closed door," Hayden added, continuing to pet the little girl. He breathed deeply. "I'm just relieved there was no one else in there." The building was going up quickly, even as they poured a ton of water on it.

"What the hell is that about? Maybe one of the dogs pushed it closed," the chief added.

"Or someone locked them in there," Hayden offered as he looked over the group of people gathered around the perimeter to watch the proceedings. "The building was under renovation. There were building supplies on the floor of the living room. It fits with our theory about the other fires." And fortunately this wasn't one Kyle was working on, so maybe he wasn't the target. He was going to be relieved about that.

"And the fire is too damned hot. Something was used to set it," the captain said before turning away to direct some of the other teams. The fire was dying quickly now, and the guys continued dousing it. Finally, as animal control arrived, the captain declared the fire out, and the teams cleared up their gear.

"What do we have?" a woman with expressive eyes and dark skin asked as she approached. A name tag on her lapel read Lilly.

"I found both of them inside," Hayden explained as Danton brought over the other dog, using a rope as a collar and leash. The bulldog mix seemed calm and nonaggressive, which was good. "The chief said the neighbors reported that they're strays." He petted the little girl's head, and she licked his fingers. God, this was one adorable little dog.

"We can take both of them," Lilly said.

Hayden looked the little one in her huge eyes and shook his head. "Is it okay if I give you my information?" He didn't want to let her go.

"Of course," Lilly replied, and Hayden got his phone, still holding the dog.

Do you like dogs? he sent to Kyle and then snapped a picture of the pupper and sent it as well.

The response was almost immediate. *Yes, I do. My father never let us have pets. He was too cheap to pay for the food.* It was followed by a sad face, and at almost the same time, Kyle hearted the picture.

"Is it okay if I keep her? I'll get her to a vet," Hayden said.

Lilly beamed.

"I'll house this one," Danton piped up, petting the powerful dog's head as his tongue lolled in puppy ecstasy. "We'll give you contact information so if anyone comes forward to claim them you can get in touch with us."

Lilly grinned. "You boys have made my day. Usually these calls end up with us taking them to a shelter. So yeah, you can foster the dogs. Let me get the paperwork."

"What is this, a fire company or a dog adoption agency?" Chief Marks asked with a teasing smile. "You guys get this taken care of quickly and then get back to work. Hayden, go on home, and thanks for your help. Enjoy the rest of your day off." He hurried away to take care of business, and Hayden filled out and signed the paperwork. He and Mitzi—she looked like a Mitzi to him—rode back to the station on the fire truck with Mitzi firmly in his arms.

He transferred her to his truck, and they made a stop at PetSmart for all the needed supplies. Kyle was home when he arrived, and Mitzi took to him right away. She ran through the house like it was some kind of jungle gym before settling next to Kyle on the sofa.

"She's a real sweetheart," Kyle said, just before she jumped up and raced to the back door. "And a smart one too."

"I can take her out," Hayden offered.

"I got it," Kyle said and put the leash on Mitzi. Hayden watched as Kyle treated the little thing like she was the Queen of Sheba from the way he spoke to her. Once she had done her business, she pranced inside, and Kyle gave her a treat before lying on the sofa once more. "I need to go to another job. I finished the one this morning, and I want to get this next one done."

"What about George?" Hayden asked.

"We're starting demo tomorrow," Kyle said. "I got a special breathing mask, and so far everything has been good."

Hayden sat as well, and Mitzi jumped up between them before curling up with her head on Hayden's knee, big eyes watching him like she was afraid she was going to be put out at any minute.

"How can anyone just abandon a sweet little thing like her?" Kyle asked, gently petting her back.

"I don't know." Hayden pulled out his phone. "I need to find a vet so I can have her looked over and he can make sure she has her shots." She licked his hand, and Hayden fell more deeply in love. He smiled, and when he lifted his gaze, Kyle's face was soft and gentle, his eyes wistful. When their gazes met, Kyle's expression shifted, growing more intense and maybe even heated. Kyle drew closer, and damned if he didn't lick his lips. Hayden did the same without thinking, his throat drying and his breath coming more quickly.

Mitzi shifted and stretched out, pressing against both of them. "Are you a couch hog?" Kyle asked, and she curled up, her head on her front paws.

Hayden swallowed hard, watching Kyle, who looked back. In a way, it seemed like he was seeing Kyle for the first time. Okay, so he knew this was probably a bad idea, but Kyle drew him, and as much as Hayden tried to pull away, every time he saw the guy, caution seemed to fly out the window.

Hayden forgot about the phone in his hand as Kyle drew even nearer.

Suddenly Mitzi stood and raced to the window, barking like crazy as she jumped on the arm of the chair, tail wagging. That interruption pulled Hayden back to the present. "What's out there?" Kyle asked as he got up to check the window.

Hayden found the number for a veterinarian he knew and dialed it. "Mitchell, it's Hayden Walters. I was at a fire scene today and rescued a dog."

"Do you want to bring it to the shelter?" Mitchell asked.

"No. I'm fostering her until someone comes forward. If not, then I'm keeping her." He went to where Mitzi had settled down, still looking out the window.

Kyle left the room, and Hayden lightly stroked Mitzi's back to soothe her. "She's a real sweetheart. She probably needs her shots and stuff."

"Bring her in at three and I'll check her out," Mitchell said. Hayden thanked him before hanging up.

"What's going on?" Hayden asked when Kyle returned, an older man with a scowl following him. "Kyle?" he asked when he saw the depth of darkness in his features.

"This is my father, Winthrop," Kyle said, and Hayden's lips formed an O, but he didn't say anything.

"I see you got a dog," Winthrop said as Hayden picked up Mitzi. "You know how I feel about them." Like the entire world should do his bidding—what an ass.

Mitzi growled and glared at Winthrop, baring her teeth, ears pointed back like she was ready to leap out of Hayden's arms at any second.

"What are you doing here?" Kyle asked. "It's Hayden's dog. He's a firefighter, and he rescued her from a burning building, just like he did for me a few weeks ago, in case you give a damn." Kyle's father didn't react. "What are you here for?"

Winthrop straightened, looking to his son and then to Hayden with eyes that would have been at home on a turkey buzzard—dull, deep, and hard as hell to read. "I came to see if you might have come to your senses. Your mother and sister miss you…."

Kyle shook his head. "Bullshit," he spat.

"Don't talk to me like that."

Kyle snorted. "This is my house, and I will speak any way I like in it. You, on the other hand, will be nice. As long as you're under my roof, you'll obey my rules." Hayden wondered how many times Kyle had heard that growing up. "I'm calling bullshit. Why are you here? What is it you hope to get?" Kyle was suddenly wound tighter than an antique clock.

"I came here to see if you had reconsidered your life. Your mother and I raised you to be a—"

Kyle cut him off. "A what? A carbon copy of you?" Kyle accused. "Well, I'm not and I never will be. Jesus… what did you think? That I would leave and be somehow more miserable than I was living at home with you?" Kyle sat down, and his father looked like he was going to sit as well. "Don't. I didn't offer you a chair, so you can stand. Remember how you used to do that whenever we wanted to ask you something? You'd sit all comfortable and make us stand so we'd know who was in charge." Jesus, Hayden had no idea the kind of home life Kyle had grown up with, but he was sure getting a glimpse of it now.

"I think I have my answer," Winthrop said, but he didn't turn to go. Hayden wondered if he should leave the room, but Kyle looked at him, his gaze pleading, and Hayden stayed where he was.

"More games. I'll ask once more. What is it you came for, and no more BS. We've already had this conversation years ago, and it ended with me being thrown out. Remember? What I want to know is, what has changed? Why are you here? Just say it and then go." Kyle's now laser-sharp gaze zeroed in on his father and didn't shift. Mitzi growled once more, and Hayden soothed her gently. One thing was for sure—she had a wonderful sense of people. "Just say it and then you can turn your back on me once again." He leaned forward.

For the first time since coming inside, Winthrop Wilson's shoulders lost some of their rigidity and his confidence seemed to falter. "Do you need some water?" Hayden asked quietly.

Winthrop shook his head. "No. What I need is a kidney."

CHAPTER 8

"YOU WHAT?" Kyle asked, reviewing the conversation in his mind to make sure he'd heard right.

"I knew this was a mistake. You were always selfish."

Kyle ground his teeth together. "Me? You disowned me because I didn't meet your expectations, and you come here, acting as though you're the great arbiter of everything, and I'm selfish?" Kyle threw his arms in the air. "Pot and kettle, old man. Lay off the guilt, Father. You don't have any ammunition." He shook his head.

"You have kidney failure?" Hayden asked, and Kyle realized he'd asked an obvious question to give Kyle time to digest this.

"Not that it's any of your concern—"

"Dammit, get off your stupid high horse. You aren't the one in control here, so stop acting like an ass." Boy, Kyle could really dish it out, but it was hard overcoming years of parental conditioning.

"Yes," Winthrop answered more calmly. "I'm in dialysis, and they told me that will work for a period of time, but the only chance for recovery is a transplant, and the best chance is from a blood relative. Your sister and brother aren't a match, and your mother convinced me to come here and see if you would be willing to be tested."

Kyle blinked and met his father's gaze. "I'll think about it," he said gently. "That's the only answer I have for you right now." He went to the door. "Have Mother call me in a few days and I'll tell her what I've decided." He held his father's gaze, refusing to back down. "You disowned me when I came out and said some very hurtful things, and right now I don't really want to speak to you ever again. So yeah, I'll talk to Mom." Kyle opened the door and waited for his father to step out before he closed it.

As soon as he was gone, Kyle's knees felt like they were going to go out from under him.

"What the hell?" Hayden asked, setting Mitzi down. She ran over, and Kyle picked her up and gently cradled her to his chest. She licked his face and then nuzzled him. What a good little one. Kyle sat back down, holding the dog until Hayden set down a bowl of food. Then she raced over and ate like she was starving.

"Wow," Kyle breathed. "What the hell am I going to do?" Part of him wanted to cut his father off and let the chips fall where they may. That was the easy thing to do.

"I don't know," Hayden whispered. "It's a huge thing he's asking from someone he cut out of his life. If my dad asked, I'd do it. But then, my dad did his best to try to understand the kind of person I am."

Kyle stopped to think. "What's he like?"

"Dad is a man's man. He always was. Football, hunting, outdoorsy type things. He's big, gruff, and doesn't suffer fools very well. Like your dad, he thinks he's right most of the time. But...." Hayden paused, blinking. "You know those times when it was just the two of us? Well, he'd listen." Hayden sighed. "I remember when I was sixteen and really trying to figure out the hand I'd been dealt. I was scared that Dad wouldn't love me anymore. But the fact that I was gay was something I was coming to know inside. Dad was thrilled when I chose to play soccer, figuring that if I was playing any sport, it might toughen me up."

"What happened when you told him?" Kyle asked, trying not to relive his panic at the extreme disappointment and then anger that merged into near fury when Kyle had told his father.

"He was shocked, I think. But it was just the two of us, and he sat in his chair, a can of beer on the table beside him. He downed the can and crushed it. Then he turned to me and said that it was okay. That having a gay son wasn't what he would have chosen because he was concerned it was going to be hard on me. He told me that I should be the best man I could be, no matter what." Hayden lowered his gaze. "After that he went back to watching the game as though nothing had happened. I kept wondering when the big blowup would occur or when he'd get mad, but there was none of that. Dad was just the same and acted the same toward me. He never said he loved me or that he always would.

That wasn't his way. Instead, he acted exactly the same as he always had, except that he took me hunting with him that fall. He insisted I come."

"Why? Because he thought it would make a man out of you?" Kyle had done plenty of shit his father wanted him to in order to prove he was a man like his dad wanted. Doing all that shit he'd hated hadn't changed anything, and in the end his father had turned his back anyway… and now was asking for a kidney.

"That's what I thought at first, and it made me angry. But no. Dad wanted to spend some time with me. I knew how to shoot because he'd taught me at twelve. He and I were gone a week, just the two of us. We sat all day in a deer blind, just watching… and we talked. About everything. He didn't shy away from any subject. It was the most grown-up I had ever felt, and I knew that my dad spending a week listening to his gay son tell him how he felt…. At least he tried to understand. I poured everything out to him, and he listened and then would pat me on the shoulder before going back to looking out across the forest."

"Where is he now?" Kyle asked, leaning a little closer as he engaged with the story. He wished he and his dad could have been that way. As much as Kyle would have liked to have a father who spent that kind of time with him, it had never happened. Everything had to be on his father's terms, and his dad was too busy trying to control everything to listen to anyone else.

"Dad and I went hunting every year after that. Usually it was just a weekend or so, but we went. Then the summer after I graduated high school, he had a stroke. It was moderate, and he spent months in therapy. After that he wasn't quite the same, and we never went hunting again. Dad's hands shook just enough that he couldn't hold the gun steady any longer. He and Mom are in Florida now. Eventually he went on disability. Mom still works, though. She was a nurse at the hospital, but now she works for a private practice outside Bradenton. They have a pretty good life there. Mom and Dad are coming back to visit in a few weeks. The heat is too much this time of year. They have a motorhome that Mom drives, and they'll stay in a campground south of Mount Holly for six weeks or so."

"Wow," was all Kyle could say. That was about as far from his own parental experience as possible. Hayden nodded as Kyle continued lightly petting Mitzi. "I guess you got pretty lucky."

"At the time I didn't realize just how much." Hayden sighed. "You still have things you need to do?"

Kyle set Mitzi down, and she hurried over to Hayden for more attention. "I do. I'll see you around this evening." Kyle gently patted Mitzi's head before he stood and left the room, wishing he could stay with Hayden. He made him feel normal, and the unease his father seemed to throw in every direction calmed when he was around.

PHYSICAL EXERTION always enabled him to work out his frustration, but this afternoon it wasn't helping. He was doing detail work, which required more concentration than exertion, and his mind kept wandering to what his father had asked of him.

"This is really looking good," David said from behind him. "Thanks for getting this done for us." He and his wife, Arleen, were making some final changes to their kitchen. They'd had to wait for their stove and microwave to arrive before Kyle could do the last of the work. It had taken months, but now he was finishing their remodel.

"You're welcome." He finished measuring and made a note of the dimensions. He checked them again before heading outside to make the cut. "This is a really nice space."

"Arleen is happy, and that's all I can ask for," David said with his usual smile. His wife was demanding when it came to her kitchen. She and Kyle had gone over everything more than once, and they had written down all instructions so there was no misunderstanding. More than once he had been asked to rework something, but because of the notes and approval, he had added the additional costs to the job when that happened.

Kyle made the cuts he needed and returned to the kitchen with David following behind. Kyle slotted the moldings into place and glued and fastened them before stepping back. He could barely see the joins at all, which was what he wanted, the lines of the moldings perfectly straight. "I think that's the last of it," Kyle said as he looked around just to be sure.

The home had been built in the middle of the nineteenth century with not one straight wall or right angle. Kyle had made it work, and now the kitchen was stunning. The one wall of original cabinets had been brought back to life, and Kyle had made the new ones to match.

"It is. Thank you," David told him with a sigh.

The back door opened, and Arleen strode in. "All finished?" she asked, admiring her new domain.

"Yes. I was just cleaning up," Kyle answered, turning away to cough. She always wore perfume, and normally it didn't bother him, but today he couldn't seem to catch his breath. "Sorry." He forced his muscles to calm.

"I heard about the fire. Are you really all right?" Arleen got a glass of water and pressed it into his hand. Kyle took a drink, and the urge to cough dissipated. "I'm okay. Thank you." He drank some more.

"David and I have purchased a fourplex rental property on the south side, and the units need some work. Two will be vacant next month, and we were wondering if you'd like the job. The others will be done when those tenants leave."

Kyle sighed softly. "Yes. Do you know what you want to do?"

Arleen nodded. "The units are all the same, with two mirror images of the others. So we thought we'd get the supplies for all of them. The leases on the occupied units are up in four and six months. We will renew them if the tenants like, but we will renovate as part of the renewal. I want the building to be well maintained, and the units can be really nice."

"Arleen always has to have a project," David said. "I'm lucky she also has a great head for business." He tugged her to him, and she smiled with such love and care that Kyle turned away. There was nothing like that in his life, and just watching them made him ache to have it.

"I can go to McCarran Supply and see what they have. There are always good basic cabinets there for amazing prices." That earned him a smile. "We can make the units nice without breaking the bank."

"Perfect. I'll send you pictures and some basic measurements. Once we can get in, we can go to work." He and Arleen shook hands, and then Kyle finished cleaning up. David wrote him a nice-sized check for his final payment. Kyle said he'd be in touch and left the house.

Kyle paused at his truck. "What the hell?" he asked, curling his nose as he approached. He set down his tools and went back to knock on the door.

"What?" David said when he answered, and then he saw it too. "The hose is right there." He pointed. "I'll go get some gloves."

Kyle's truck was covered in brown stuff that smelled like a sewer. Kyle wasn't sure what it was, but he had a good idea. David turned on the water and sprayed the truck. Fortunately most of the gunk rinsed away. Kyle took the hose and gloves and gave the truck a good clean.

"What kind of person does that?" David asked.

The same type of person who sets fire to a building with someone in it? Kyle finished washing the nastiness away, put the hose back where David kept it, and turned off the water. "Thank you." The area still stank as Kyle put his gear away. "I'm sorry for the smell."

"It isn't your fault." David looked up and down the street. A couple of other cars had had the same treatment, so maybe this hadn't been aimed at Kyle specifically. Still, it was damned unsettling. "I'll tell my neighbors." He went back inside, and Kyle pulled out and headed home, watching in his mirrors in case someone was following him. Maybe he was being overly dramatic, but it wasn't every day that his truck got covered in crap.

Kyle parked on the street and got the hose to wash off the truck again, because the stench had followed him home. He rinsed everything down before going inside to be greeted by a bouncing Mitzi. "Hey, little girl. Has anyone claimed you?" he asked, looking at Hayden, who shook his head. "How can they not?"

Hayden sighed. "I don't know. But the vet techs groomed her for us and gave her a flea bath. She was covered. They also gave her some shots that the little princess was not happy about. She's apparently been fixed, but Mitchell suspects she's been on her own for a while, judging by how thin she is and her condition. I fed her a little more just a while ago, and I thought she could have a few treats before bed." Clearly Hayden was trying to win her over with food.

Kyle told Hayden about the job he'd gotten, as well as about what had happened to his truck. "I have no idea what it means. It could be someone playing a prank."

Hayden nodded. "And it could be revenge for something."

Kyle had thought of that. "Anyway, at least I got some more work, and I confirmed with George about starting work tomorrow, so I'm going to be busy." He sat down and took a measured but deep breath, pleased he didn't cough. "I'm no closer to figuring out what I'm going to do about my father."

Hayden nodded but blessedly didn't offer an opinion. Kyle was grateful for that. He suspected that everyone would have one, one way or the other, but this was something he had to decide on his own.

"Well, why don't you go clean up?" Hayden offered.

Kyle nodded and went to his room, where he got fresh clothes and then hopped into the shower. The hot water felt good on his muscles. He stood still, head bowed, as water ran down his back. He knew what he wanted to do—tell his father to go pound sand and leave him alone. But that was the easy answer. Things were never as simple as what he wanted. There were other things to think about. After all, this was his father, and even if the man was an ass, Kyle wondered if he still owed him something. He washed his skin, keeping his eyes closed and trying to sort through the myriad of conflicting emotions and wants. What he needed was some kind of clarity, and he wasn't getting it.

Eventually Kyle turned off the water and dried himself, pulled on comfortable clothes, and returned to the main part of the house. The table had been set, and the room smelled like heaven. "What have you been doing?" Kyle asked.

"Well, you were working, and I know your dad has made things hard for you." Hayden brought a bowl of green salad to the table and set it down next to potato salad. "It's not a fancy dinner, but I found some really good bratwurst at the store, so I grilled them and got a few fixings. It's not much more than a picnic, but I thought you could use a little home cooking."

"Did you buy the potato salad?" Kyle asked.

Hayden shook his head. "I called my mom, and she helped me over the phone." He brought over the last of the food and a couple of beers before sitting down. "She makes the best, with onion, bacon, some mustard, and other ingredients that she swore me to secrecy about." He smiled, and Kyle did the same in return.

"That's really nice. Thanks." To say it was a tough day was an understatement, and to have Hayden do something nice for him was a little overwhelming. He had to caution himself not to read too much into it. "Now I hope you don't get called away in the middle of dinner."

Hayden scowled. "You said it," he said with mock anger, then grinned. "I'm no longer on call as of five o'clock. That honor shifted to someone else, so unless there's a huge fire that needs all hands, I'm off for a few hours." He took a brat and passed over the tray. They smelled amazing, spicy and savory. Kyle took one, along with some rich mustard that he was willing to bet Hayden's mother told him to get.

Kyle's phone rang, and he pulled it out of his pocket. It was the familiar number of his parents' home on the display, without a name. He stared at it for a few seconds. It had been a while since he'd seen that number. "Home," he said.

Hayden nodded and lowered his gaze to the table, continuing to eat as though the food was the most interesting thing on earth.

Kyle sighed and then answered the call. "Hello?"

"Ky?"

He knew that voice, and he smiled before he could stop himself. "Hi, Mom," he said gently and then halted. Kyle had no idea what to say to her after that. She had turned her back just as much as his father had, simply because she hadn't stood up to the old coot.

"Oh, honey, it's good to hear your voice," she gushed and might have been tearing up. Kyle sat straighter in the chair, because not hearing his voice was her fault and her choice, not his. "Your father told me he came to see you today."

Kyle cleared his throat. "Yes, he did." He wasn't going to give an inch. "He came by the house. I just happened to be home."

"I know. I heard about the fire and that you were rescued." She sniffed. "Are you really okay?" She used the same tone that she had when he'd been hurt as a kid.

"I'm fine," he said gently. "I'm working, and my lungs are healing. I got a lot of smoke, but…." He met Hayden's gaze. "A friend saved my life."

"That's good. Look, your father said he spoke to you today about his health, and he said I should call you. I don't understand why, though." As usual, she was pretty good at ignoring what she didn't want to deal with.

"Because Dad is an ass," Kyle told her flatly. She gasped. "Don't try to correct me, because you know I'm right. He asked me to help him, and I'm thinking about it. I'm going to need a few days to consider what he requested." That was all he could say.

"How can you say that? He's your father, and he needs help."

Kyle clamped his eyes closed to keep from losing his temper. "You know why, and how he treated me. And I know what you're going to say, but don't push me. Otherwise my answer will be no, and then he can spend the rest of his life tethered to a dialysis machine. He was always part unfeeling robot anyway."

"Your father always did his best for all you kids," his mom protested.

Kyle wasn't buying it. "As long as we did what he wanted, we were fine. But I'm not going to argue about this. My father is who he is, and so am I. Right now I'm the one with the decision to make, and I won't be rushed or bullied." That seemed to give her pause. "I'll call you in a few days." Kyle ended the call and returned to the table. "I'm sorry about that."

"Your mom drank the Kool-Aid as far as your father is concerned?" Hayden asked.

All Kyle could do was nod. He shouldn't have expected anything different. She might not agree with his father, but she wouldn't stand up to him or say anything against him either. And maybe that was worse. His father's feelings were his own, and he thought they were right. His mother didn't have the backbone to think for herself. In some ways, Kyle felt sorry for her. "That's enough of them. I've had all of Winthrop and Harriet Wilson that I can stand for one day."

"I'm not going to argue," Hayden said. "I'm sorry you had to go through all that. It must have been hell when you were a kid."

Kyle sighed and figured it was best if he said nothing. Hayden stared at him through his silence, and Kyle wondered what he expected. "It was, and I took it out on the people around me. It was easier than actually accepting that my family was a dysfunctional steaming pile. It's not an excuse for how I acted, because there isn't one. I was old enough to make my own decisions. But when you're mad at the world, you don't tend to do the right thing." He ate a few bites of his sausage and wished he could put all that behind him. But nothing was that easy.

"I understand that. I was lucky I had a family who didn't care about that stuff. My mom went to PFLAG meetings after I came out so she could try to understand."

"My father tried to shut down that group at the school because he didn't think it was appropriate. Thankfully he didn't get his way, but he sure tried." Kyle remembered that fight. Outwardly he had done everything to make everyone think he agreed with his father, but inside, he'd cringed every time his dad or one of his mindless cronies said something derogatory, because he knew they were talking about him and they didn't know it. Now he knew they wouldn't have cared if they had.

Mitzi raced from under the table to the back of the sofa to peer out the window. Then she raced to the back door before hurrying back to the window, tail wagging.

"What is it?" Hayden asked and went to take a look. "Come on, silly girl. There's nothing there." Hayden returned to the table, and they finished their dinner.

Hayden cleared the table, and Kyle put the left-overs in the fridge and loaded the dishwasher. "That was really good. Thank you." He was feeling a little kicked around, and Hayden's kindness meant a lot.

"Do you want to watch something on TV?" Hayden asked.

"No." He was too anxious and unsettled to sit still. "I was going to go out for a walk through the park. It might help clear my head." Kyle got the leash Hayden had bought and snapped it onto Mitzi's collar. "I'll take her with me."

Hayden hesitated, like he wasn't sure he should come, and then joined him. "If you want to be alone, I get it."

Kyle shrugged. "I honestly don't think I'm going to be good company… but sure." He unlocked the door and stepped out into the evening air. Mitzi pranced on her leash next to him, and Hayden walked quietly. Kyle watched straight ahead, half paying attention and half trying to figure out what he was going to do.

"I hate that they've backed me into a corner. If I get the test and I'm a match, then I'm obligated to do it or I look like an uncaring dick. Yet I'm supposed to do this for my cold-as-hell father who doesn't give a damn about me. If I say no, I'm the guy who let his father die, and if I do this, then I'm having surgery and putting my life in danger for a man who turned his back on me." Kyle hated being put in this position.

"I get it," Hayden said. "Now that I've met your father, I can see the man is a real ass. I think I'd feel the same way." He paused. "Maybe think about yourself in ten years. What will you regret doing or not doing?"

Kyle stopped walking at the entrance to the path that served as the back way to the park. "That's just it—I don't know. If the positions were reversed, my father might do it for me, but he'd have a list of conditions a mile long first. I know he would. Winthrop Wilson never does anything without something in it for him." He turned to face Hayden. "But before you ask, I don't want anything from him. Not a damned thing." Mitzi jumped against his leg to get Kyle's attention, and he started down the path. "I won't do that. There is no way that I can be like him."

Hayden nodded, and in that second, Kyle knew what his answer was. It didn't matter what his father had done. Kyle was a better man than him, and he'd do what was right, period.

"Did you just decide?"

"Yes. I'm going to have the test, and we'll see what happens from there." What Hayden had said did help, because no matter how he felt about his father, this was the decision where he could live with his reflection in the mirror each morning. "But I'm only going to agree to the test for now, and I'm going to take a day or so before telling my mother. She and my father can wonder for a while."

Hayden snorted, a completely inelegant noise. "It sounds to me as though you know their game."

Kyle shrugged. "I do. I learned to play it pretty well while I was living with them. If I were to answer too quickly, then they would think that I'd easily do what they want, and the requests will become more frequent and serious." Not that this one wasn't serious or important, but with his father, Kyle knew he had to try to keep as much control as he could. "I hate having to play these games, but you've met my father."

"I most certainly did," Hayden said. They continued walking with Mitzi enjoying herself. When they returned to the house, Kyle unlocked the door, and they went inside.

"You should let me do that," Kyle said, but Hayden motioned him to sit while he got them something to drink. Kyle sipped his coffee, his thoughts wandering from the situation with his father to Hayden, because, damn... he moved with a smooth grace that had Kyle wondering if that ease of movement would translate to the bedroom. He knew he shouldn't have these kinds of thoughts. They were destined to go nowhere, but then again, it didn't hurt to daydream a little.

"Are you all right?" Hayden's voice cut through his wandering thoughts.

"Huh? Sorry...," Kyle mumbled.

"I was asking if you wanted dessert now or later. My mom talked me through some of her famous chocolate mousse with raspberries. We can have it later if you like."

Kyle nodded and was flooded with an image of him eating chocolate off Hayden. Once that flashed in his mind, damned if it didn't decide to take up residence. The temperature in the room inched upward, and Kyle shifted slightly in his seat, hoping Hayden didn't notice as he adjusted things to be less obvious. Kyle was really getting himself into trouble, and he needed to put the brakes on these sexy ideas. "I think that would be great."

"We could watch a movie," Hayden offered.

"Sure. I can look to see what's available. What sort of thing to do you like?" Kyle went to the living room and brought up the selection of movies. There were thousands, and he looked through them, trying to find something good.

"Oh, *Latter Days*," Hayden said as the title flashed on the screen. "I watched part of that on TV a while ago." He sat next to Kyle on the sofa and put his feet up. Kyle started the movie and settled in, trying not to look over at Hayden every few minutes to check his reaction, especially when one of the main characters in the movie, Christian, had his shirt off, because Kyle had a hard time not comparing Hayden to the actor—and the actor definitely came up short.

CHAPTER 9

THE TELEVISION was definitely there, and Hayden watched the movie, but he was also hyperaware of Kyle. Every time he moved, Hayden glanced over at him. When he shifted on the sofa, Hayden swore the sound echoed off the walls of the room, but he knew it was only in his head. Mitzi climbed onto his lap to curl up, and he absently stroked her back as the movie built to its romantic crescendo. He gasped and held his breath at the restaurant scene, tensing as Kyle tensed. When he rested his hand on the cushion next to him to give it a break, Mitzi huffed in a "Why aren't you loving me?" way, but heat burst through him when his fingers encountered Kyle's.

He turned away from the big screen TV, meeting Kyle's wide, intense gaze. Hayden didn't pull away but wriggled his finger slightly, rubbing it against Kyle's hand. Then he turned back to the television without saying a word, leaving his hand where it was.

The movie ended in a lovely piece of romantic movie afterglow, and Hayden closed his eyes. "Jesus… I hope I don't have to go through that much shit to find someone," he breathed.

Kyle's breath hitched. "Maybe you already did." The finger stopped moving, and then Kyle turned his hand over, sliding his fingers on Hayden's palm. "I was terrible to you in high school because I was so fucking messed up. But I kept watching you, and…." He inhaled sharply. "I kept wondering about you."

Hayden swallowed hard, his heart pounding; the air around them seemed to crackle and fizz. "I always knew you hated me because I was gay and I was an easy target."

"I did. But I hated the world, and you above everything, because I couldn't have you or anyone like you." Kyle's hand tensed, and then he tried to pull away, but Hayden held on tightly.

"Just say what you want to say," Hayden said, keeping that physical connection, like if he let it break, then this moment would pass and never come again. "I used to watch you all the time back then. Yeah, because I had to make sure I knew where you were, but also because… well…." He bit his lower lip. "Because you were hot back then. So I'd catch glimpses of you in gym when your shirt rode up or when you were covered in sweat and it stuck to you like glue." He felt as though he was confessing the worst sin imaginable.

Kyle continued watching as the credits rolled for the movie. "I didn't have the guts back then to say what I really felt, and I covered it all up with this roiling soup of anger and frustration. I didn't know how I was ever going to figure out how to see the other side of it, and you looked like you already had. And then I started noticing you, and it made me more confused. It was so much easier to just hate you than to be honest with you… or myself." Kyle finally looked at him. "I want to say this for the record. Back in school, you were the brave one. You had enough courage to be the person you were. I was the coward who hid who I was under a pile of attitude and behind a façade."

Their gazes met, and Hayden let himself see beyond their pasts. It was more than time to let all that go. What he needed to do was figure out what he wanted—a difficult thing while his entire body thrummed with passion. Kyle didn't move an inch, but Hayden found himself drawn closer, pulling nearer without conscious thought. And maybe that was for the best. Maybe he should turn off his head and just follow that voice from deep inside telling him to go for what he wanted. "Kyle, I…." Hayden's throat ached, it was so dry. He licked his lips and drew closer. Mitzi shifted before jumping down off his lap, the sound of her nails clicking on the floor growing fainter, but Hayden barely noticed. His attention zeroed in on Kyle. He didn't dare move his hands. It felt like this moment was a thread of glass and if they moved it would shatter.

It was Kyle who lifted his hand, sliding his fingers through Hayden's hair and around the back of his neck. Hayden slid his eyes closed a second before his lips touched Kyle's for the first time, and stars supernovaed in the darkness. He pressed closer, desperate for more, and damned if Kyle didn't part his lips. Hayden finally allowed himself to move, slipping his arms around Kyle, pulling him closer, deepening the kiss that already felt like perfection. Hayden refused to let doubts and worries enter his head. He kept them locked away in their box, at least for now.

"Oh hell," Kyle whispered.

Hayden stayed close. "Tell me about it," he said softly. "Things just got complicated."

Kyle chuckled. "I was thinking that things just got real… fast. I always wondered what that would be like. I used to think about it sometimes when I was alone, in the dark. I'd wonder all kinds of things. It was the one time and the one space where I could allow myself to go wherever I wanted." Kyle kissed him again, pressing against him. Hayden let himself be pushed back on the pillows.

Kyle was like a live wire whose coating had been stripped away, and now his power was free to go wherever it wanted. Then he pulled away, gazing down at Hayden with those huge brown eyes filled with a blaze of heat that had sweat breaking out all over Hayden. Kyle slowly sat back up. "I don't want to make a mistake."

"Then don't," Hayden said softly before tugging Kyle back down, their lips finding each other. The television returned to regular programming, and Hayden fumbled for the remote and hit the button. Then quiet descended in the room, broken only by their soft moans and heavy breathing.

A sharp bark from Mitzi made them both stop. Hayden turned to where she sat next to the sofa, watching them. "Are you jealous?" Hayden asked. "I take it you want all the attention."

Mitzi raced over to the chair and jumped up onto the back to look outside. Her tail stayed still, and she glared.

"Let me see what's going on," Hayden said, and Kyle backed away. Hayden reluctantly sat up and went over to the window as the backyard lights flashed on. Hayden looked out but saw no one. Mitzi growled, jumped down, and raced to the back door, barking and scratching to get out.

"It's okay, little miss, I'll take a look." Hayden pushed Mitzi away before opening the door and hurrying outside. He looked out over an empty yard, but when Kyle opened the door again, Mitzi raced out between his legs. She took off along the side of the house, barking as she went. Hayden hurried after her, afraid that if she got away, she wouldn't be able to find her way back.

As he hurried out into the alley, a dark figure turned the corner with Mitzi after him. Hayden chased both of them.

Mitzi growled as Hayden approached the man. She had his pant leg in her mouth now, snarling like a dog much bigger than she was. As he drew closer, Hayden recognized Kyle's father. "What are you doing here?" Hayden demanded, soothing Mitzi until she let go. Then he picked her up while she continued to growl at Winthrop. "Why are you here? Stalking Kyle? Trying to see what your son is up to? Maybe scare him a little? Have you been hanging around here?" He stalked closer.

Winthrop backed away. "He's my son." As though that explained everything.

"Yeah, but the way he tells it, you weren't much of a father. What kind of parent turns their back on their kid for any reason?" Hayden shook his head. "Go away. And don't be surprised if Kyle tells you to go to hell. I know if I were in that position, I'd have nothing at all to do with you again, let alone agree to give you anything… like a kidney." Hayden held Winthrop's gaze.

"How long have you been doing this?" Kyle asked as he came up behind him.

Winthrop swallowed but didn't answer.

"How long, Dad?"

"I knew where you lived, and…," Winthrop mumbled.

"So kicking me out of your life wasn't enough. You had to find me and, what? Try to scare me?" He drew closer. "Are you a firebug too? Did you try to burn out my clients and kill me?" Hayden shifted Mitzi and put an arm around Kyle.

"Of course not. How can you think that?" Winthrop's eyes widened, and his shoulders slumped.

Kyle glared at his father. "I don't know. I wouldn't have thought you'd cut me out of your life, but you did without a thought, so who knows what you're capable of." Kyle leaned against Hayden. "How long have you been coming here? Weeks? You'd sneak into the yard and make the lights go on just to try to scare me? What did you think—that I'd ask to come home?" Kyle shook his head. "That I'd ask for your forgiveness?" He turned to Hayden.

"Hey," Hayden said softly. "Come on. Let's go back to the house." Mitzi continued snarling and squirming to get out of his arms. She hated Kyle's father, that was for sure.

"Go home," Kyle told his father. "And stay away. I don't want to talk to you or see you." He turned, and

Hayden went with him, shielding Mitzi from seeing Winthrop. At least then she calmed down.

"Well, that's one mystery solved," Hayden said. "But I don't get why he'd suddenly take an interest in stalking you."

Kyle shrugged. "I don't understand it either, but it doesn't matter. He can go to hell as far as I'm concerned. He tried to kill me and probably intended to try to burn down my house around me."

Hayden got Kyle inside and to the sofa, then locked the doors, even though he was pretty sure Kyle's father was gone and probably wasn't coming back. Then he placed Mitzi on Kyle's lap and went to get some water for him. "If it's any consolation, I don't think he was the one who set the fires."

"How do you know?" Kyle asked.

"I don't. But when you mentioned the fires, he looked completely confused. Your father may be a lot of things, but I somehow doubt he's responsible for that." An idea skittered around the back of Hayden's mind, but he couldn't quite pin it down. He felt like there was something he was missing, yet he had no idea what it was yet. "I'd have expected him to get defensive if you accused him of setting the fires and he was responsible. But he didn't. He just looked confused."

Kyle sighed and leaned against him. "At least I know I wasn't going crazy. There was someone watching me and hanging around. I guess the last person I suspected would be my father. He kicked me out years ago."

"Maybe it's something as simple as he needed to figure out how to get to you to ask about the kidney and he wasn't sure how to do it," Hayden offered.

"He could have tried the phone," Kyle offered, and Hayden knew he was right. There had to be more to it than that, but Hayden had no idea why anyone would act that way. It didn't matter much. Kyle's father wasn't going to be hanging around any longer; Hayden was pretty sure of that.

"Just do your best to relax," was all Hayden could think of to say. "At least we know who was triggering the lights and watching you." He tried to put the best face he could on the situation.

"You're right. But I'm starting to wonder if my dad is losing it. If he's going into kidney failure, maybe it could be affecting his mind."

Hayden gasped. "Damn, you're right. We learned about this in medical training. He's on dialysis, and if he isn't following his diet…." Hayden could see it now. The way Winthrop scratched his hands and arms while he and Kyle talked to him. How pale he was. "I bet you things are already building up inside him that he can't control. Look at how pale and yellow he looked the other day. He's in bad shape, and I bet he's obsessing about what's going to happen to him and thinks you're his only hope. He will only survive on dialysis for so long. He can't go very far, has to be on a machine four hours at a time three days a week, and even then, it isn't perfect. His kidneys aren't cleaning his blood constantly, so as soon as he's done with treatment, the toxins begin to build up."

"How do you know all this stuff? Do they give you that kind of training?" Kyle asked.

Hayden shook his head. "Grandpa. My mom's dad. I loved him so much. He and I did everything together until I was eight years old. Mom used to say that we were inseparable." The ache was still there if he thought too much about it.

"Did he die?"

Hayden nodded. "Kidney failure, just like your dad. He was on dialysis too, and they tried to get a donor. They tested everyone in the family, and the only one who was a match was my mom, but she wasn't viable because of other health issues. I remember Grandma telling me about what he went through, because I asked over and over. I even remember asking if I could go with him to dialysis to hold his hand. But I was too young and they wouldn't let me." He'd done his best to push away those memories. "Grandpa died when I was eleven."

"Let me guess—he was a different person by then," Kyle said.

"Yeah. No more trips to the zoo together, no more baseball games. Instead we played cards, and he sat in a chair most of the time, trying not to scratch himself raw from the buildup of phosphates." He swallowed hard. "I still miss him sometimes." Like a lost tooth. He was an amazing man, and Hayden had always felt special when he was with him. Grandpa never judged him, not even when he borrowed one of Grandma's needles and thread and sewed himself a pair of the worst-fitting pants on earth. "Grandpa was the first person to take me aside and tell me that it didn't matter what I wanted to be or who I was, that he'd always love me forever." He tried to remember how many rough days in school that he'd held on to that memory like a talisman.

"You told your grandpa that you were gay at eleven?" Kyle asked.

"No. I didn't have the words back then. But I think Grandpa did, and maybe he understood things that I didn't. He told me I should be myself and that if anyone didn't agree with that, they could go to hell. That was exactly what he said." He would love his grandpa forever because of it.

"You were lucky to have someone like that," Kyle said softly. "I know I never did. 'Be a man, don't act like a sissy.' Everything was under a microscope. I was the youngest son, and my father wanted me to be the person he thought I should be. It didn't matter that I had no interest in that. I played football because he insisted on it. I was terrible at it, but quitting was out of the question. That is until I managed to get caught smoking and was kicked off the team."

"I remember the rumors and indignation flying through the school. I thought you got what you deserved. But you did it on purpose."

"Of course I did. I never smoked in my life. Yuck. But there was a zero-tolerance policy for that sort of thing, and I knew it. Dad couldn't fight it, and I could stop getting beat all to hell every single practice and game. And it was one way for me to have some control of my own life. Dad went ballistic, but that was it. Eventually he calmed down." Kyle shrugged and leaned back on the sofa, closing his eyes. Mitzi sprawled out between them, and Kyle reached over her to take Hayden's hand. "I wish more than anything that I had had the guts to be like you back then."

"We all take our own path." As much as Hayden wished his school years had been easier, they'd helped make him into the person he was now. "And I am who I am. So why hide it?"

"See? You knew shit back in high school that I was so clueless about. I used to think I was smart and knew everything. Turned out I didn't know shit," Kyle whispered.

"Let's put that behind us. It's in the past. Neither of us is in school now, and if I can be frank, we have more important things to worry about. There's still someone out there who is setting fire to buildings in town. And your father's health is obviously worse than we originally thought, and I suspect that your family is most likely going to employ the full-court press to get you to help him." Hayden hated to say it, but judging by their behavior so far, he could see it coming.

"I know," Kyle said softly. "I used to dream that they would see the error of their ways and want me back. But now I hope I never see or hear from any of them again." He stood slowly. "I'm going to bed. I have to start work with George tomorrow, and all of this is just more than I can take right now." He left the room, and Mitzi followed him, then returned after a few minutes.

She climbed onto the sofa and lay on Hayden's lap, looking up at him every few minutes like she was wondering why he wasn't going to bed too. "Let's take you outside, and then I'll give you a treat." He'd hoped Mitzi would sleep in the bed he'd bought for her, but she disabused him of that notion when Hayden climbed into bed after cleaning up and she jumped right onto the bed and curled up next to him. Hayden placed her in her doggie bed, and she stayed there for about three minutes before joining him once again, then settled down and curled up. Hayden was too tired to keep playing the bed game with her, and if she was good, he didn't really mind.

He didn't sleep well, though. It seemed Mitzi chased things in her sleep, and Hayden wasn't particularly comfortable. After a few hours, he got up to get something to drink. When he went past Kyle's partially open door, he heard a soft cry. He peered in and found

Kyle half under the covers, lying on his side, leg thrashing as he hmphed softly. "No…," he said distinctly before shooting upright.

"Kyle," Hayden said gently. Kyle blinked at him. "Are you okay?"

He wiped his forehead and gasped. "God," he breathed. "I…."

Hayden stepped into the room and sat on the edge of the bed. He was in only a pair of boxers, but it was the middle of the night and the room was dark. "What happened?"

"I had this dream where my family decided that since I had chosen not to give my father a kidney, they were going to take it anyway." He gasped and seemed to be trying to breathe normally. "They held me down on the table and grabbed a butcher knife. That was when I woke up."

"Okay, that isn't real, and it's never was going to be. They may try to guilt you into it, but that's the limit of their power, and they only have it if you give it to them." Hayden lightly stroked Kyle's arm as Mitzi ran into the room and leaped up on the bed. Clearly she wasn't going to be left out. "Just relax and try to go back to sleep."

Hayden intended to leave the room, but Kyle pulled him down, and Hayden didn't resist. He ended up resting on Kyle's second pillow, right next to him.

Kyle watched him, blinking, then licked his lips before closing the distance between them. "Don't leave me alone." Kyle kissed him and scooted right next to Hayden, sliding a leg between his.

Hayden paused, cupping Kyle's cheeks in his hands. "Are you sure this is what you want? A lot has happen—"

Kyle cut off Hayden's words, pushing him back against the bedding. Hayden smiled as Kyle pressed down on top of him, body vibrating. Apparently this was exactly what he wanted, and Hayden had been thinking about this for long enough that he didn't have the will to bring it to a stop. He had decided to move beyond the past, and damn, Kyle felt amazing in his arms.

Mitzi jumped down off the bed, probably out of self-preservation, and Hayden groaned as Kyle slipped out of the last of his clothes. Hayden managed to get rid of his boxers, kicking them off. Skin to skin, nothing between them—it was a glorious feeling that Hayden wanted to hold on to for as long as he could.

Hayden slipped his hands down Kyle's back and over the curve of his sweet ass, gripping his cheeks as he devoured his lips. He wasn't going to hold back as waves of pleasure washed over him. Hayden had wondered what this would be like for a while, even when he knew he shouldn't. Now that he had Kyle in his arms, he was going to hold him for as long as he could.

Maybe both of them would come to their senses, and maybe they'd decide this was a mistake, but for right now, Hayden intended to go with it as instinct took over. He held Kyle tighter, reveling in the hard muscular curves of his body.

"Hayden," Kyle whispered, pulling back, his eyes wild, lips already swollen. "Damn…."

Hayden rolled them on the bed and pushed Kyle against the mattress, sliding their cocks alongside each other. Kyle groaned deeply, the sound only adding to Hayden's desire. He wanted this more than he had wanted anything before, and now it was coming true. "Just go with it."

"Yeah," Kyle gasped, shaking in Hayden's arms. It was sexy just how excited Kyle was—and that Hayden was the object of his desire.

Hayden lightly sucked on Kyle's ear. "What do you like?"

Kyle stilled, looking at Hayden like he was crazy.

"Hasn't anyone asked before?"

Kyle shrugged.

"What? Did you just do whatever they wanted and hope it felt good?" Hayden smoothed the hair out of Kyle's eyes. "You know you have a voice and you get to say what you want." Hayden started to understand just how deeply the crap with his family had been drilled into him.

"I guess I like normal stuff," Kyle said.

Hayden stroked his cheek. "You can say the words. There's no need to be shy," he said softly, holding Kyle tighter. "You have been with guys before?"

Kyle chuckled. "Yes, I have. And things were pretty good, if you must know."

"But they never found out what you wanted. Did they just assume that you liked what they liked?" Hayden asked with a wry grin. "Well then, if you don't want to tell me, then I'll just have to figure it out." He smiled and slid downward. "Let's start here." He lightly sucked at the back of Kyle's neck, not hard enough to raise a mark, but enough to have Kyle moaning softly. "You like that."

Hayden tried his nipples, plucking and sucking, but Kyle didn't react much, which was fine. Not every guy liked the same things. Continuing downward, he found a spot just above Kyle's hip that left him panting for air. Damn, that was an amazing sound. "Hayden…," Kyle gasped.

He pulled away, letting Kyle catch his breath. Damn, he loved the way Kyle looked in the bed, laid out on the sheets, cock straining toward his belly button, eyes half shrouded, chest heaving as Hayden opened for him. The sight took Hayden's breath away. "You know, there are times when it can take hours to figure out what someone likes." He ran the tips of his fingers down the center of Kyle's chest and then his belly, following the ridges of the muscles, then ran them around his navel before sliding his fingers around Kyle's cock, gripping his hard length, and stroking slowly.

"Jesus," Kyle moaned.

Hayden leaned closer, continuing his motions as he took Kyle's lips in a hard kiss. "If this is new to you, I have to wonder what kind of selfish guys you've been with before." Hayden kissed him again, loving how overwhelmed Kyle seemed. Hayden got the idea that no matter what Kyle said, he hadn't had a lot of experience with guys. That alone was sexy as hell. There was nothing sexier than the way Kyle seemed to lose himself in Hayden's touch. When Hayden broke the kiss, Kyle's wild eyes gazed up at him in what Hayden could only describe as disbelief. "Let's see, what should we try next?" Hayden asked in a wicked tone before sliding down Kyle's taut body, his lips blazing a trail to his cock. Hayden slid his lips around Kyle's length and slowly sucked him in.

Kyle gasped and clutched the bedding as Hayden took more and more of him, watching Kyle's eyes as they darkened. He slowly pulled away before sucking him deeper once again, bobbing his head slowly just because that seemed to drive Kyle even wilder. Maybe Kyle's previous lovers had all been selfish pricks. Hayden wasn't sure, but Kyle seemed surprised at these sensations, and Hayden wanted to completely blow his mind.

"Hayden, I'm—" Kyle stammered as Hayden took him deeply, his nose buried in the soft curls at the base.

He pulled back. "It's okay." He didn't want Kyle to climax, not quite yet. He still had plenty to show his new lover.

CHAPTER 10

KYLE FELT like a fool. He'd hoped that Hayden wouldn't realize that he hadn't been around the block. Part of him wanted to disappear, and he probably would have tried to hide himself if Hayden wasn't making him feel so damned good. Even after coming out, he hadn't gone searching for other guys because he knew his family was waiting in the wings to hear things about him.

"Oh God," Kyle whimpered as Hayden slipped back and then rolled him over. He licked his way down his back, parted Kyle's legs, and slid his hands between them. The way Hayden held him, his hands never still, nearly drove Kyle over the edge. It was like he never stopped, and Kyle grew more and more inflamed.

Hayden hummed as he played Kyle's body, making it sing in ways he never knew possible. "Is this what you like?"

"Yes," Kyle croaked, clamping his eyes closed, letting his mind float on the ripples of ecstasy. Very few people had touched him in such an intimate way, and even his ex, if he could call him that, had been much more reticent when it came to such things. Hayden, on the other hand, didn't hold back, and that was heaven. "Don't stop," he breathed.

Hayden leaned close to his ear. "I won't, sweetheart. No way am I going to do that... not until you come."

Kyle quivered, and Hayden held him, keeping Kyle grounded while he drove him out of his mind.

When Kyle rolled over, Hayden lay on top of him, tugging on his lips with his kisses as Kyle held Hayden's firm ass. "What are you made of, rocks?" Kyle asked.

"I work out hard to stay in shape," Hayden told him, shimmying his hips until Kyle groaned again, his cock sliding along Kyle's. "After all, I have to carry people out of burning buildings."

"Don't remind me," Kyle said.

Hayden smoothed the hair away from Kyle's face once again. "I'll carry you out of a burning building, up the stairs, or wherever you want me to."

"Your impression of a caveman?"

Hayden kissed him again, sliding his hands down Kyle's side. "Oh no. It's my fireman routine, and I'll do it as many times as you need me to." He winked, and Kyle kissed Hayden hard, losing himself in the sensation. He rolled his hips slowly, matching Hayden's tempo. Kyle let himself get carried away.

"Aren't we going to...," Kyle began, arching his back, "you know... the anal part?"

Hayden nuzzled his neck. "Not this time. I think it's best if you and I take things slowly. Besides...." He shimmied his hips, and Kyle rolled his eyes, hanging on. There was no hurry for anything, and damn... in a few minutes, Kyle reached the point where he couldn't control himself any longer and tumbled in a mind-blowing release that left him breathless and hugging Hayden to keep himself in one piece.

"Oh God," Kyle mouthed as he tried to catch his breath. He wondered if he'd done the right thing and half expected Hayden to slip out of bed and return to his room. When he did climb off and leave the room, Kyle stared into the empty doorway, sighing to himself. This was the story of his life—a quick fuck and then they were gone. Not that he'd had all that many partners, and the one that had stayed the longest had never made him feel the way Hayden had. Part of him felt so alive, and yet he was still alone.

"Scoot over," Hayden said as he walked naked back into the room. He used the cloth he was carrying to clean Kyle up before returning it to the bathroom. Then Hayden slipped under the covers, and Mitzi hurried back into the room, jumped onto the bed, and pranced at their feet, making sure her spot was just the way she wanted it.

"Okay, settle down already," Hayden told her, and Mitzi watched them both before curling into a ball. "That's a good girl." Hayden rolled over and tugged Kyle to him.

"I thought you'd gone back to your room," Kyle whispered.

Hayden guided him, and Kyle rolled over. He spooned Kyle from behind, his arms sliding around his waist, holding him close. "Whatever kind of guys you've been with in the past… you need to know that I won't treat you that way."

Kyle closed his eyes. "Maybe I don't deserve to be treated any better," he said into the darkness. "I did a lot of shit in my life. You know that."

"And maybe you were surrounded by people who treated you the way you thought you should be treated. But that's bullshit. Maybe if you had been supported instead of pressured to fit in, you'd have been a hell of a lot happier. Now go back to sleep. We both have to go to work tomorrow."

"What are we going to do with Mitzi?" Kyle asked. "I don't like the idea of leaving her here alone all day. What if she thinks she's been abandoned again?"

Hayden chuckled and pressed even closer. "It will be okay. Why don't you stop home at lunch to check on her and take her for a walk?"

"Okay." He fell asleep, content and happy. But in the back of his mind, Kyle was well aware that just when things were going well and he was happy, that was usually the point where everything went to hell.

"WE GOT a lot done," George said that afternoon as he looked around Hayden's apartment. They'd moved most of the furniture into the bedroom. George had rented a floor sander, and they got the old wood smoothed out and stained. They took out the old, falling-apart kitchen cabinets, and once the floors were finished, they'd install the new ones.

"Yeah. I thought we'd finish the floors in here, and then we can demo one of the other units. Keep the work flowing." Kyle liked George, and there was quite a bit of work to do in these units. The sooner they got done, the sooner George and his wife, Connie, could rent out the units again. But that meant Hayden would be returning to his apartment as well. That wouldn't be for a while yet, but still, Kyle liked having Hayden around. He was truly a kind person, and somehow he'd managed to help Kyle with his family. Kyle simply felt stronger with Hayden around, and the sex was great.

"Sounds like a good idea," George said as he stretched his back. He was probably about seventy, with white hair and a strong build. Kyle got the idea that he was used to doing all of the work himself but just wasn't able to any longer. "And if we run into a roadblock, we can always start painting. I really want these units fresh and clean. It's been quite a while since we've been able to really update them, and they need it." He began gathering up the tools. "I really appreciate your help."

"It's no problem." Kyle closed his toolbox. "I need the work."

George nodded. "I heard about the fire. That's a real shame." He picked up his toolbox and placed it in one of the empty apartments. Kyle did the same, and George locked it up. They had been using the upstairs landing when working with their tools so they didn't get marks on the floors. "I'm heading down the street for a beer. Do you want to join me?"

"I'd like to, but I have to get home. Hayden is still working, and the dog needs to be let out. Hayden found her at a fire just yesterday. They're trying to find her owners, but is it wrong that I hope they don't? She a sweetheart, and I'd really like to keep her."

George clapped him on the shoulder. "Nope. We have a golden, and Ally is pretty special. Connie and I have always had dogs. When we had the shop on the main floor, we used to bring her in. She'd spend her days with us." His expression was wistful. "There's just something about a dog. Ally's old now, and she doesn't get around like she used to. But she's great company, and Connie says that when she goes, we're getting another." He didn't seem unhappy about that idea.

Kyle started down the stairs to street level and waited for George at the bottom. He closed the door, and George locked it.

Sirens sounded in the distance, growing closer, and Kyle turned as a fire truck screamed down the main street. He couldn't see if Hayden was on it, but he raised his hand just in case and lowered it as they raced past.

"I worry about him," George said.

Kyle nodded. "Me too. But then, he's the one who pulled me from a burning building." He shrugged. "Hayden is one of the most capable people I've ever met." He just seemed to know what to do.

After saying good night to George, Kyle hurried home. The first thing he did was put Mitzi on her leash and take her outside, where she immediately did her business, and Kyle gave her a treat. Once back inside, he checked the house and praised the sweet girl again because she hadn't had an accident. "I think Hayden is out with a fire," he told her and sat on the sofa. Mitzi jumped up and climbed onto his lap to get the attention she thought was her due.

He sent Hayden a message to see if he was okay and to ask when he'd be home. Not that he expected an answer right away, but Hayden would see it when he could. Kyle was about to set down his phone when it rang. The number wasn't familiar, but it was local. He half expected it to be spam, but he answered it anyway.

"Kyle?"

"Bella?" Kyle asked. He'd only spoken to his sister a few times since his father had turned his back. "What's going on?"

"It's Dad. He needs your help," she said levelly. "He's getting worse, and the dialysis is only doing so much for him. I tried to help, but I'm not a match. Jason isn't viable, and I'm so worried." She sniffed. Kyle wondered if they were crocodile tears.

"Do you know he was stalking me?" Kyle asked.

"No way. You have to be imagining it," she countered.

Kyle huffed. "I found him. He was watching me here at the house in the evenings sometimes. We caught him." He wasn't sure which tack to take. "You know what he did and that he hasn't spoken to me in years. I know he thinks I'm the instrument of the devil and all—"

"That's bullshit. I always thought so," Bella said. "But you know Dad. He thinks he knows everything and acts like judge and jury."

"I don't see you standing up to him." Instead, she was here pleading his case. "You and Jason do whatever he says and nod your heads like good little minions."

Bella didn't argue, which surprised him. "He's going to die unless you help him." There was the guilt, his family's greatest weapon.

"I already made an appointment for the blood testing." Kyle had called at lunch and arranged it. "But beyond that, I can't say what I'm prepared to do." He was scheduled for the draw tomorrow. The tests would take a few days. "He's asking a lot from someone he kicked out of his life. And before you say anything, remember he was the one who burned that bridge, not me." He was tired of all of them. "I'll call Mom once we know if I'm a match or not, and then we can go from there. But I'm not making any promises."

"He's our father," Bella said.

"Maybe he's your father, but mine turned his back on me some time ago. I wasn't good enough to be his son. But now that he wants something...." Kyle was only getting angrier. "Just back off, Bella. I'll get the test, and we'll see how things go from there. But I will say that if you all want me to help, it's time everyone started acting like it. The entire family feels that I should just do what you want. I'm my own person and I have feelings, and mine are just as valid as the rest of yours. I'm not going to change for any of you. And if you want my help, then you need to see about changing some of your backward thinking." He was really getting fed up.

"I never thought Dad was right," Bella said softly. "Not when it came to you."

At least that was some progress. "I'll be in touch, Bella." Kyle ended the call and set his phone aside. The only person he hadn't heard from was Jason, and it wasn't going to make any difference at this point. Yes, Dad needed a kidney, and at this point in his life Kyle had an extra. But what if he needed it down the road? Maybe his father's condition was hereditary. Kyle had no idea, and all of that was going to need to figure into his final decision.

"Come on, girl, let's get you something to eat," he told the dog, and she hurried to her bowl and waited for him. Kyle measured out her food, and she gobbled it down. He hated that she seemed so worried that someone might take it or that this was her last meal.

Hopefully she would come to understand that he and Hayden would feed her and that she wasn't going to go without.

When she was done, Kyle put her leash on and they went for a walk around the block. Mitzi smelled all the doggie smells and left her own mark for the other dogs. By the time they got back, Hayden's truck was pulling into the drive. Hayden got out to meet them, his expression serious. "Put Mitzi inside. We need to go."

"Where?" Kyle asked.

"To my building. I just heard from Dirk. Someone broke into the empty store on the ground floor and tried to set it on fire."

Kyle could barely feel his legs as he got Mitzi inside. He rode with Hayden downtown, where they parked across the street from the fire trucks. The street was filled with emergency vehicles.

"I'll be here if you need me," Kyle said, figuring there was no need for him to get in the way. "Hayden, tell them that the floors in your place are wet, and if they don't need to go up there, to stay out."

He nodded and hurried off. Kyle bounced his foot on the floor of the truck. Someone really *was* after him. If there had been any doubt, this clinched it. He'd worked on the building for only a day and someone had tried to set it on fire. Shit, what kind of sick person was this?

Hayden hurried back across the street and pulled open the door. "It didn't get far. It seems they tried to get in through the back but didn't make it into the store itself. They tried to set the fire in the garage, but a neighbor called, and Dirk's company got here fast. He said the fire is out, and there doesn't seem to be any damage upstairs since the garage area is off the back and not directly under the apartments."

"That's good news for George and Connie." It didn't change the fact that someone had come after Kyle once more.

"Dirk said he checked out the pictures of anyone watching and was going to turn them over to the police. They said they'll investigate, but I think you need to contact them."

"I know. I'm the only link between the fires." And after this became general knowledge, no one was going to hire him for fear they'd be next. Kyle couldn't blame them. "I'm screwed until we find this guy." And he had no idea who it could be.

"I agree. I'll be sure to let Dirk know what's happening, but you might want to call the department when we get home. Let them know that you're worried and that you'll do anything you can to help." Hayden didn't mention it, but Kyle figured that would also help allay suspicion that he was the arsonist. God, that was all he needed on top of everything else.

"I will." He sighed. "But what the hell am I going to do?" They headed back toward Kyle's house.

"I don't know. I doubt George is going to fire you, especially since now he's going to need your help making some of the fire repairs."

Kyle didn't know if that was true. "What if they come back, and this time they set all of downtown on fire?" He knew he was being dramatic, but he was becoming more worried by the second. He had a mortgage to pay, and his family sure as hell wasn't going to be any support. The more he thought about it, the more frightened he became, even as they arrived at Kyle's.

"Let's not panic. The police and the fire department are both going to be on this. Dirk and I are already looking into other fires that might be related. We need as much information as we can get if we're going to find this guy and douse his ass." Hayden drew closer. "But we need to find out who might want to do this, and I'm afraid those answers lie in your past."

Kyle nodded. "Maybe we can call Rachel and the three of us can sit down and have a 'Kyle was an asshole' party."

Hayden scowled. "I don't think we have to go to that length, but maybe Rachel can help us." He sat down at the table. "Everyone has enemies. We can't live our lives without upsetting someone. Not everyone we hurt is crazy enough or has enough pent-up anger and resentment to go around setting fires."

"I know that," Kyle snapped and wished he hadn't. Hayden was only trying to help, but Kyle was on edge. "But how do we find them? I haven't screwed anyone over or ruined a job for anyone. I always give reasonable estimates and work hard to be done on time. I never overcharge, and other than Ellen, whose house burned down because of me, I don't know who would be that angry. Anyway, I suppose that doesn't count, because she would have had to have burned her own house down to hurt me, and that seems a little extreme." God, he was running a mile a minute and not making sense.

"Okay. But let's think. Yeah, you were a dick in high school, but that was a decade ago. So let's leave that behind. Is there anyone you took a big job from?" Hayden asked, but Kyle didn't know. It wasn't like there was a list of who was bidding on what. He provided estimates, and the homeowners made their choices.

Hayden leaned forward. "Here's something. How about your family? Is there someone who could be trying to get to them through you? That could be a stretch, but it's something we can look at."

Kyle shrugged. "You met my father. He's an ass. There are lots of people who would want to get at him. Anyone he got the better of in a business deal. My father doesn't care about anyone other than himself."

"How do we find out? Maybe this really has little to do with you. I know that some folks in town know what your dad did, but it can't be common knowledge, and your dad has been hanging around and stopping by the house. If whoever is behind this is watching you, then it would look like you and your dad are close and he's spending time with you." Hayden had a point. They wouldn't know the conversations they were having or the dynamics between the two of them.

"We'll need an insider."

"Is there someone in the office you could speak with?" Hayden asked. "Someone you know personally?"

It wasn't a completely off-the-wall idea. "You know, if we want to check it out, I know just the person we need to talk to. Diane, his assistant. She's been with him for years. She might know anyone who would hold a grudge against Dad, and I know where she'll be tomorrow."

"Why?"

"Because it's trivia night at Molly Pitcher, and she's there every week."

CHAPTER 11

HAYDEN WAS tired. Call after call had worn him out, and one had come in just before his shift ended, so he stayed, which meant he was running late.

"I'm here, and I know we need to go," he told Kyle as soon as he came into the house. "Let me clean up fast and we can leave." He hurried up to the bathroom and got undressed, then stepped into the shower. He washed quickly and got out, then hurried to the room he'd been using wearing only a towel.

"You know, we could always go next week," Kyle said, drawing closer as Hayden turned to face him. "A week's delay would be a small price." His expression already had Hayden's motor running, but Hayden needed to remember what was important.

He let the towel slip away and started to dress. "We need to keep our heads in the game." He paused and took a step closer to Kyle. "But don't worry. I'll make it up to you when we get home. I promise." Damn, he loved the way Kyle swallowed and his eyes widened. The flush that spread across his cheeks was adorable, and all that was missing were just-kissed lips and maybe a hickey at the base of his neck. Then Kyle would be absolutely perfect. Hayden pulled his gaze away, finished dressing, and followed Kyle downstairs.

Mitzi pranced up to him, and he gave her some attention while Kyle explained that she had been walked and fed. So at ten minutes before six, they headed for downtown and managed to get a parking space a block from the brewpub, which was some sort of miracle. "I hope she's there," Kyle said.

"Think positive," Hayden told him as he pulled the door open. The taproom was packed. "Is she here?"

Kyle nodded. "At that table right there."

"Perfect. She's by herself. Go on up to her and say hello. See if she'll ask you to join her." Hayden hoped it would be that easy, and it seemed it was.

"Diane, this is Hayden, a friend of mine," Kyle said, and Hayden shook her hand before taking a seat.

"Have you ever played this trivia before?" Hayden asked. "How does it work?" The announcer was making introductions, and answer sheets were being distributed as Diane gave an overview. Then she turned to Kyle.

"How have you been? I haven't heard anything about you from Winthrop lately." She sipped her beer with a smile.

"I'm doing well. I'm operating my own business as a contractor. I saw Dad a few days ago." Hayden noticed that Kyle gave no details. "I haven't been by the office in quite some time. I always loved that. You used to sneak me candy when Dad wasn't looking." They shared a conspiratorial grin, and Hayden let his gaze wander through the room.

"He was always so hard on you kids," Diane said with a half scowl that lasted only a few seconds. Still, it was enough to show that while Diane may have worked for Kyle's father for years, she didn't always agree with him. That was promising. "I always kept some treats in my desk. Your brother used to go right for that drawer, but you and your sister always asked."

Kyle chuckled. "That sounds like Jason. He always felt like everything was his due." He shrugged, and Hayden watched the two of them interact. Diane drank her first beer and ordered another as the trivia caller began his questions. Kyle paid attention and knew some of the answers. Hayden did as well, but Diane was a master and had most of them. She wasn't as good with the sports questions, while Kyle knew quite a few of those answers. As the trivia wore on, Diane had another beer and became more talkative.

"How are things at work now?" Kyle asked her.

Diane shrugged. "It's okay. Your father is slowing down, and he's been trying to bring Jason into the business. He's different from your father, less cutthroat. He grew up better than I thought he would. I think he'll keep the business running well, if he decides to give up firefighting and take over."

Kyle leaned over the table. "I was never involved. Was Dad really that underhanded?"

Diane shook her head. "He skirted the law. I'm sure of that. I'm willing to bet he didn't always disclose things when he was selling a property. He'd sometimes pretend he didn't know, and it's hard to prove that sort of thing after the fact. Real estate is a tough business, and your dad was always really good at it. He had a sense of when an area was going to come up. He'd buy the properties, fix them up, and either rent or resell them. More than once he started the revitalization of various sections of town."

She sounded proud, and maybe Kyle's father had a right to be. They were here for information, and as long as Kyle kept Diane talking, they might get a piece of what they needed.

"Did Dad ever really hurt anyone? Like, ruin them or anything?" Kyle asked. "You hear stories and stuff. I know Dad was tough, but I never thought him that cruel."

Diane shrugged. "Business is business. He used to say that win-win deals were rare, and often when somebody won, someone else lost. Your father made sure he came out a winner most of the time."

After a short break, the caller returned to the questions, and their conversation grew quiet for a few minutes.

"Did Wilson ever get burned out of a building?" Hayden asked. "I'm a firefighter in town," he added to explain his interest.

She thought a minute. "I think so. One of his rentals burned, maybe ten years ago. I don't think anyone was hurt, and Winthrop ended up taking the insurance settlement, tearing the building down, and selling the lot to the neighbors. In the end he came out well, but the renters always said that they were owed something for their things. They apparently didn't have insurance and lost everything. It was sad, but not your father's fault." Hayden made a mental note to try to look up the details of that fire.

Diane answered the next group of three questions and finished her beer. Kyle made sure she wasn't driving and then ordered her another. "I think I remember that. It was on the south side, right?"

"North East Street and Louther, if I remember. The buyers of the lot used it to increase the size of their yard. It's really pretty now, and you'd never know about the fire."

The announcer wrapped up the questions and went through them once more before taking a break.

"It all worked out in the end, I guess." She drank some more of her beer and then excused herself to go to the bathroom.

"That was interesting," Hayden said as he grabbed one of the pieces of quiz paper and made a quick note about the fire. "Maybe one of the renters or their kids still holds a grudge."

"I'm not sure this is the way to find anything. Why not just go after my father? They could set fire to his buildings and burn him out directly. Why go through me to get to him? It doesn't make any sense," Kyle said.

Hayden had to admit that was probably true, but something told him there was more to this than they knew. "You may be right, but it isn't going to hurt to look into this and see if there's anything. And we got a night out regardless." He flashed a smile, and Kyle gave him one in exchange.

When the server returned, they ordered some food and asked Diane what she'd like. Then they settled in for the revelations of the answers.

They only missed one, and their team was the big winner of the night, which meant they got their food order comped. Diane was pleased, and she ate as she finished her beer. Then, once she settled her tab, she said goodbye and walked out of the tap room and into the night, while Hayden looked into Kyle's eyes.

"What do we do next?" Kyle asked, probably referring to the investigation.

"Finish eating, pay our bill, and then go home." Hayden leered slightly and loved that Kyle's cheeks pinked up. He was so damned responsive, and that did great things for Hayden's ego.

"About the person trying to burn me out of my living," Kyle clarified as he rolled his eyes.

"I don't know." Hayden paused. "I say you go back to work with George and put a bug in his ear about maybe installing some cameras in the foyer and in the back garage area. Our arsonist failed this time, but with you still working there, maybe he'll be dumb enough to try again. If we get him on camera, then maybe we can burn him."

"Funny," Kyle deadpanned. "Don't quit your day job."

Hayden snickered. Yeah, it was a bad joke. He was coming to really enjoy that smile and was going to miss it and Kyle when he moved back into his apartment. Hayden never would have believed it, but staying with Kyle might have been one of the best things fate had ever thrown his way. He had largely gotten past the mess that was high school, and he could look at Kyle in a whole new way. He didn't have the dagger of his past hanging over him, and Kyle was a better person than Hayden would have ever thought possible. On top of that, they seemed to get along, and Hayden was even developing deep feelings for him.

And the sex… that was a whole mind-blowing subject of its own. Jesus. Kyle might not have had much experience, but he was a fast learner, and he made up for his shortcomings in raw enthusiasm. But it was more than that. Hayden was coming to think of Kyle so differently… more like a lover, a friend, and that was both frightening and exciting at the same time.

He finished his food and paid the check for both of them. The crowd in the taproom thinned out a little, and they left with the post-trivia group while others were just coming in. At the truck, they climbed in, and Hayden drove back to Kyle's, noticing that there weren't any lights on around the back. Things on that front were quiet, and the lights were still functioning. But he still made the rounds of the back, making his presence known.

Kyle brought Mitzi out, and she jumped around his legs until he petted her thoroughly. Then she did her business and led Kyle back inside. "I keep trying to think of who might want to get even with me," Kyle said softly.

Hayden understood but had no insight. He slipped off his shoes and settled on the sofa while Kyle went upstairs, with Mitzi following. Hayden took the opportunity to call Rachel for a little outside insight.

"What's going on? Have you two killed each other yet?" she asked.

"No," Hayden growled.

"Are you sleeping together?" she pressed, and Hayden didn't answer quickly enough. "You are. I

knew it." She cackled. Hayden ground his teeth, wishing he hadn't called in the first place. "So spill. You
like him, don't you?"

"Rachel…," he cautioned.

"Oh, come on. There's nothing wrong with the two
of you getting together. He's a nice guy, and he grew
up like the rest of us did." She had that scolding tone. "I
don't think you called so I could give you grief, though.
What's going on?"

"Other than someone setting fire to the places
where Kyle is working?" Hayden asked. "So far we
have three confirmed, including one attempt just the
other day. But we don't know who would do that. I
mean, it's one thing to not like someone, but it's another to set fire to buildings."

Rachel sighed. "Do you remember Jimmy
Kergan?"

"Yeah…. He was nuts."

"And he used to like blowing things up. You remember the time he nearly blew his hand off at the
homecoming game?"

"Weren't he and Kyle friends?" Hayden asked,
wondering where Rachel was going.

Rachel gasped. "You really are out of it. Jimmy's
dad and Kyle's dad were going to go into business
together. Some big deal that fell apart. It was a huge
deal, and old man Kergan had to declare bankruptcy. It
made the papers a few years ago. That section of land
that they're just now building a hotel and condos on to
the north of town was involved. Took years to sort the
whole thing out."

"And let me guess. Winthrop came out smelling
like a rose while everyone else got screwed?" Hayden
supplied. "That sucks, but how does that involve

Kyle?" It was clear that Winthrop had left a trail of bad
feelings in his wake, but that didn't explain this fixation
with Kyle.

"I don't know. Maybe it doesn't. Maybe he holds
Kyle responsible somehow. Jimmy wasn't the brightest
bulb on the string."

"Okay. Maybe the police can look into him.
They've already talked to Kyle, and I suspect they'll
want to again. Maybe this can help." It wouldn't hurt to
look deeper. "Maybe this is a 'sins of the father' kind of
thing." His gut told him it wasn't. There was something
closer to home. This arson seemed personal, especially
with how these buildings were being targeted. Someone wanted Kyle to hurt, and they didn't care how they
went about it.

"Or maybe this is one fucked-up sicko whose
behavior makes no sense at all. I watch these crime
shows, and the experts are always digging in to try to
explain, like, Jeffrey Dahmer's behavior. I understand
that we always want to know why someone does shit,
but maybe they're just sick and do shit because it turns
them on. Maybe this guy doesn't like Kyle and likes
to see things burn, so he's combining his passions and
getting off on it."

"I suppose it's possible. But it's more personal
than that. Kyle started work in my building, and the
first day, this guy tried to torch it. There's more to this
than we know. The thing is, the trigger doesn't have to
be that big… at least anywhere but the arsonist's mind.
Something small gets blown out of proportion, built on
over time, and suddenly Kyle is responsible for everything that's wrong in life." He could understand that.
Hayden had held on to his anger with Kyle for a long
time.

"Then the answer is easy. You need to look for the arsonist in a different place. Where they are likely to strike next. If they tried and failed to set fire to Kyle's latest workplace, what do you think they'll do?"

To Hayden the answer was simple. "Try again."

"Either that or take the fight even closer," Rachel supplied, and that was exactly what Hayden was afraid of.

HE TALKED to Rachel for a while longer before checking the doors and outside. Then he turned out the lights and went upstairs. Hayden figured Kyle was asleep and didn't want to disturb him, so he went to the room he'd been using and got undressed.

"Is something wrong?" Kyle asked at his door just as Hayden was about to pull back the bedding.

"No," Hayden answered and turned around. "I didn't want to wake you."

"Like I can sleep," Kyle said softly. Mitzi came in and stood in front of Hayden as if to say, *Why aren't you in bed?* She looked alternately at both of them, then wandered out of the room and turned to look back.

"We're coming, little girl," Hayden said softly. He took Kyle's hand. "I'm not mad or anything. I just wanted you to be able to rest."

Kyle tightened his hold. "I'll sleep if you're with me." And just like that, Hayden understood the trust that Kyle had placed in him. It touched him, and he didn't take it lightly. That kind of faith was precious and had to be met with care.

"Let's go to bed." He lightly kissed Kyle's hand, and they went down to his room and climbed under the covers. Hayden lay awake as Kyle got comfortable and

Mitzi did her bedtime prancing. Then he lay staring at the ceiling. He wondered how in the heck he was going to keep Kyle safe. It truly seemed that someone was intent on getting to him and that over time they were getting bolder, escalating to the point that they might come for Kyle directly. Hayden wasn't an investigator, he was a fireman, but if he was going to keep Kyle safe, then he would have to figure out what was happening before the arsonist grew too bold to keep at bay.

Hayden knew that time was not on his side. The fire at Ellen's, the one he had rescued Kyle from, had been less than two weeks ago. What they believed had been the first one had been months earlier. The time between had shortened dramatically, and that meant that the next one could be just a few days or even a matter of hours away.

That thought kept Hayden awake for much of the night, just listening for any sounds from outside. At one point he fell asleep with Kyle in his arms, and if he hadn't been so damned worried, he'd probably have taken the time to remember just how lucky he was at that particular moment... and how amazing it was to have someone trust him completely enough to sleep in his embrace.

MITZI BARKED repeatedly and raced from the room. Hayden glanced at the clock—five fifteen—before jumping out of bed. He grabbed Kyle's robe, which had been draped over a chair, and headed downstairs. "Call 911," he yelled as light danced in one of the side windows. "Kyle!" he yelled.

"Already calling," Kyle answered as Hayden raced outside.

Hayden grabbed a hose from the front of the house, turned on the water, and was already spraying when he turned the corner. Flames engulfed the side of the house. He sprayed at the base of the wall and up the side, blasting what seemed to be the source of the fire. Steam rose, and he continued wetting down the blackened wall.

Sirens grew closer as he continued working, keeping the water on the dying fire. Running the hose upward, he let the water run down the wall, clouds of steam rising from the hot siding.

"Nice robe," Dirk said flatly as he turned the fire hose on the remaining flames, dousing them quickly. He ran the intense spray of water up and down the wall, cooling it off and then saturating the ground at the foundation.

"Smartass," Hayden said. "Thanks for getting here so fast."

"No problem," Dirk told him. "Now I'd say you should probably go inside and put on some pants before you talk to the chief. You don't need to be flashing him your bare ass or anything." He laughed and returned to his work. "It looks like it was just the siding. You got the flames before they even reached the eaves."

"That was because of Mitzi." Hayden turned to where Kyle stood, dressed only in a pair of jeans, holding their own little fire alarm. "Are you both okay?" Hayden hurried over, pulling the robe tighter around him. He didn't care about the chief or anyone else as long as Kyle and Mitzi were okay.

"Yeah. We're fine. Is it out?"

"Yeah. The siding is burned and will need to be replaced, but the flames didn't get any farther." He gently stroked Mitzi's head. "This one is a great alarm. She

knew something was wrong and alerted us right away."
It would definitely have been worse without her. In five
or ten minutes, the flames could have taken the entire
side of the house and even entered the attic. If that had
happened, then chances were the house would have
been a total loss. But he didn't mention that to Kyle.

"Is it safe to go back inside?" Kyle asked.

"Give us a little while just to make sure the structure is truly okay, and then you can return. I'll also
make sure you get a report on the fire for your insurance company. Call them first thing in the morning."

"And tell them what? That some lunatic tried to set
my house on fire?" Kyle snapped. "What the hell am I
supposed to do?"

"The men are checking that the house is safe. It
was closed up, so the damage is only on the outside,
and it was confined to this wall. It didn't have a chance
to really get started, so we believe that the charring is
superficial, but Dirk and the guys want to be sure. As
for the insurance company, you'll get a copy of the
fire report. It will state that they believe that the fire
was intentionally set but that you are not suspected in
any way. That will allow things to move forward with
them." Hayden slipped an arm around Kyle's waist.

"But what if he comes back?" Kyle held Mitzi as
a shield, and she settled in his arms like she knew he
needed comforting.

Hayden knew neither he nor Dirk had answers for
that. His place was out of commission, or else he'd offer to have Kyle stay there with him, though that building had already been attacked as well. He waited while
the others finished up.

"Go pack a bag for yourself and get together some
things for Mitzi. I'll be inside in a few minutes. Don't

worry, I'll take care of everything." The need in Kyle's eyes touched Hayden deeply. It wasn't sex, but something deeper, like Kyle would be lost without him.

"Damn. Lee looks at me like that sometimes," Dirk muttered. "Is he going to be okay?"

"God, I hope so. Whoever this is needs to be found, and fast. They're out of control. What's next? Burning down the entire town to try to get to him? Setting fire to three of his workplaces and now his house, the last three in the past few weeks.... I'd say the obsession has become nearly uncontrollable." Hayden knew he needed to stay alert and quick on his feet if he was going to be able to protect Kyle and Mitzi.

"We're going to clear things up here. Go find a hotel for the night and get him away from here. We'll finish up, and I'll come get you when we're done."

"Thanks," Hayden said and went inside the house. Some of the guys were still inside, and he heard one up in the attic. Hayden went to his room and packed a small bag for the night. Then he found Kyle sitting on the side of his bed, a bag at his feet, Mitzi in his arms.

"When is this going to end?" Kyle asked.

Hayden sat next to him and lightly touched his arm. "I don't know. But the guys and I are all doing our best to find this guy. The police are involved, and Dirk is going to call in this incident. Right now we need to get you and Mitzi to a hotel so we can all get some rest tonight. George is going to need your help tomorrow, and I'm going to need some sleep so I can try to help Dirk figure this out."

"Guys," Dirk called from downstairs, and Hayden patted Kyle's leg.

"I'm going to go see what he needs and find us a hotel room. Bring your things downstairs and put them in
the truck." He gently hugged him and then left the room.

"What's going on?"

"We've checked the house and it's sound, so no
issues there," Dirk told him. "The neighbor across the
street says he saw someone. Gavin is an ER doctor, and
he was coming home from the hospital when he saw a
man walking up the drive to the side of the house. He
said he thought it might have been Kyle. But it obviously wasn't since you two were in bed." Dirk pulled
out his notes. "He said the guy seemed to be dressed in
dark clothes, maybe jeans and a dark shirt. The street-
light cast a lot of shadow. He was pretty sure it was a
man, and he thought he had light hair because that was
more visible than the rest of him."

"Of course he didn't think anything of it until the
fire started," Hayden explained to himself.

Kyle came down the stairs carrying the bags, with
Mitzi behind him. "What's this about Gavin?" he asked.

"He saw someone," Dirk said. "We have a vague
description, but we know some things we didn't before.
The arsonist is male, with light hair and about your
build. Gavin thought it was you when he first saw him."

"What about Jason?" Hayden asked. "He looks a
lot like you."

Kyle groaned. "Why would he be doing this? Jason has everything he could want. He's Dad's favorite,
and might take over for him, and if Dad passes away,
he'll get everything he ever wanted. I have to say he
does have the same build as I do, but his hair has darkened over the years and is more brown than anything."

Dirk stepped forward. "You grew up with him.
Was he fascinated by fire?"

Kyle shrugged. "Not that I remember. But he and I didn't run in the same circles. He was more interested in being the one in charge all the time. But maybe we'll have to pay my brother a visit and see what good old Jason has been up to. God, I hate even crossing paths with him." Kyle sighed and checked his phone. "I forgot that I should be getting the results of my blood test tomorrow." He leaned against Hayden's shoulder and yawned. Hayden held still and made a few calls to find a hotel.

"We're going to be at the Courtyard downtown. They have a room, and they'll take dogs, and that way we can be close to the house." Hayden thanked Dirk, who agreed to lock everything up. Hayden got Kyle into the truck with Mitzi, and they headed out. The rest of the night was going to be unsettling as hell, but at least they should be safe enough… for now.

CHAPTER 12

KYLE WOKE with a start and grabbed for his phone. It was a little before eight, and he had eight messages already. He was scared at what they might be.

One was from his mother, saying she had heard about the fire and was asking if he was okay. Kyle answered that he was, wondering if maybe some sort of motherly affection was overcoming her need to do as his father wished. The next message was from George to say that he would meet him at nine to see about repairing the fire damage and to continue work on the units. That was a relief. Two were from Rachel, who wanted to know if he was okay. Apparently word really got around quickly.

"What are you doing?" Hayden slurred as he rolled over.

"Answering messages and seeing if the world fell in while I was sleeping." He drew closer to Hayden just so he could touch him. Kyle answered George that he'd be there and Rachel that he, Hayden, and Mitzi were all fine. One of the other messages was a reminder of a dentist appointment in a couple weeks, and the last was from his sister, asking him to call her when he got a chance. Kyle said he'd call and set the phone aside. "I have a few minutes before I have to get up. I thought I'd stop by the house to see the damage in the light of day, and then maybe I can figure out what it's going to take to repair it." At least he could do the work himself.

Mitzi came up for her good-morning hello and then jumped off the bed and headed for the hotel room door. Hayden pushed back the covers and pulled on his pants, immediately depriving Kyle of the view of his spectacularly dimply butt. He added a shirt and slipped his feet into shoes before getting her leash. Then they left the room, and Kyle lay in bed alone. Awake now, he got up and went into the bathroom, where he stepped into the shower.

Hayden and Mitzi had returned by the time he got out of the shower. "Now there's a sight." Hayden smiled at Kyle in only a towel. "If I had more time, I'd definitely take advantage, but Dirk messaged and asked me to stop by his station on my way to work. He thinks he may have a lead and has requested a meeting with the police as well. I'll let you know what we find."

Hayden tugged off the shirt he'd thrown on to take the dog out and pulled Kyle close, skin to skin, chest to chest, their combined heat warming Kyle clean through. "I'll see you after work."

"What about the dog?"

"I'll take her with me to the station. She can spend time with the guys. A few others have brought their dogs to the station from time to time, so it will be okay." Hayden didn't step away. He held Kyle in his arms, hands stroking down his back. He even hazarded a slide lower, letting them roam over top of the towel, cupping his ass until it fell away.

The feelings seemed reciprocated as Kyle unfastened Hayden's pants and they slid to the floor. He hadn't put on anything under them, which Kyle thought was sexy and made his blood race. Kyle couldn't take his eyes off Hayden's gorgeous body. Hayden kicked the pants away, lifted Kyle off his feet, and deposited him on the bed, kissing him desperately. Mitzi took cover under a chair as Hayden growled the sound of bone-deep need. "Just a minute," he groaned and raced to where he'd left his kit. He returned quickly, and Kyle stroked himself, legs hanging off the bed, as sweat broke out on Hayden's forehead.

"This isn't how I planned this," Hayden growled and slicked his fingers, leaning over Kyle as he kissed him, slipping first one and then a second finger inside him. The stretch and the burn were exquisite.

Kyle moaned, filling the room with energy that crackled between them. Hayden plunged deeper, Kyle writhing on the bed from the sheer force. They were short of time, and Kyle would have loved to take hours, but Hayden fished for the condom he'd dropped on the bedding, ripped open the package, and rolled it onto his cock.

"Yes," Kyle groaned, and Hayden slowly sank into him, filling Kyle completely. Hayden went carefully, but Kyle tugged him forward, the battle between the two forces only ending with Kyle's panting breathing and Hayden seated deep inside.

The sight of Hayden above him, stretched out, with muscles long and lank, skin glistening, eyes wide, hair mussed, lips plump from kissing, set Kyle wild with passion. Hayden drew back and plunged deep again, and Kyle's breathing increased. Once Kyle began to shake and quiver with excitement, Hayden let his passion free.

"Oh God, don't stop," Kyle chanted as Hayden took everything Kyle had to offer and gave his entire self.

"I won't," Hayden promised and went deeper and harder, shaking the bed as he sent them both on a rocket to outer space. Hips snapped, skin slapped, and Hayden leaned forward and kissed Kyle hard, his movements becoming shallower and more desperate. They needed each other as much as they needed air to breathe, and as Kyle's pleas grew more intense, Hayden drove them both high until Kyle came unglued, gasping as sweet release overtook him, which sent Hayden tumbling into his own, falling forward into Kyle's embrace.

They held each other in quiet afterglow, content to simply be together until their bodies separated and Hayden pulled away.

As much as Kyle would have loved to stay in Hayden's arms, he knew they both had to get going. Still, when Hayden jumped into the shower, Kyle followed him, and they cleaned up together, Hayden's strong hands roaming over him until Kyle had to leave before he jumped him again and they were both late.

By the time he and Hayden checked out and left the hotel, with Mitzi in Hayden's arms, Kyle had calmed down, and once they returned to the house for his truck, they went their separate ways, with Kyle anxious for the day to be over.

KYLE AND George worked hard all day and got all of the units demoed and ready for paint and cabinets. They also got a coat of finish on the floors in Hayden's apartment and fixed the minimal fire damage. George said it wasn't worth putting in a claim to the insurance company, but he did make sure the police knew about the costs and work involved so when the person was caught, the damages could be assessed.

"Are you up for a beer?" George asked as they locked everything up tight at the end of the day.

"Yes," Kyle answered without hesitation. "I'll meet you at the corner as soon as I get all my tools put away." He carried his toolbox out to the truck and placed it in the bed box, then locked that as well.

The sun shone brightly, and Kyle took a minute to bask in the summer heat. He closed his eyes, letting the warmth warm his face. When he opened them again, Kyle locked the truck doors before heading down to the Hanover Grill.

A man stood near the corner, watching as he approached. He looked familiar, but Kyle couldn't figure out where he knew him from. He seemed intent on watching Kyle, but then he turned and got into a Toyota and backed out of the parking space. Maybe it was because of everything that had happened lately and he was making too much of little things, but a zing went up Kyle's spine, like he'd just seen a ghost or something.

The man was about Kyle's build, with blond hair and intense eyes. He wondered if he'd just been staring into the eyes of the arsonist. He turned as the dark blue car exited the lot and made a left down the alley toward Bedford. Then he hurried toward the front of the bar and went inside.

George sat at one of the tables, and Kyle took a seat across from him and ordered a local microbrew they had on tap. He also sent a message to Hayden to let him know where he was. It seemed so natural to include Hayden in his plans, yet the more work they did on his apartment, the closer they came to the day Hayden moved home.

When the server brought his beer, Kyle drank half of it in a few gulps.

"Slow down," George cautioned. "What's got you spooked?"

"I may have just seen the guy who tried to set your place and mine on fire. I don't know for sure, but he matched the description of the guy who was seen last night, and it freaked me out. It's like I should know him, but I don't."

"Don't think about it too hard and it will come to you," George told him. "I ordered a plate of wings for us. I figured you could use some food, and with the way you downed that beer, you'd better get something in your belly." When the server brought the wings, he and George shared them as they talked about the next steps in their various projects. "I added a camera to the back of the building today."

"Good idea." Kyle knew this wasn't over. "What about the stairwell to the apartments? We could get one and put it in easy enough."

George hummed. "I don't think I can do that because it would interfere with my tenants' privacy. They don't need me knowing when they're coming and going. But...." He set down a wing bone. "Maybe it wouldn't hurt for now. Once we catch this asshole, I can remove it. There isn't anyone living up there anyway, so it would be protecting my property."

"Yes. And as long as you disclose the camera to your tenants, you could keep it there. It would be an added security measure." Kyle wasn't sure George would want to do that, but at least he could have the option.

"I'll think about it." George licked sauce off his fingers before taking another wing. "McCarran Supply is going to start delivering the cabinets next week, so everything needs to be ready at that time."

"No problem," Kyle said. "We're well ahead of schedule." He ate a few more wings and finished his beer. "I should probably get going. I have to see how much damage the fire did to the siding and see if I can get the supplies to repair it." This was another thing he didn't need on his plate. George nodded as Kyle stood up, and then Kyle returned to his truck and went home.

At least no one seemed to have been there. The south side of the house was black, with char lines running all the way up to the peak of the roof. As Kyle stood looking up at the mess he was going to have to clean up, Hayden pulled into the drive, followed by another pickup truck. Three men climbed out and began unloading supplies.

"What's going on?" Kyle asked as another truck pulled up in front of the house.

"I told some of the guys what happened, and Lee here stopped by. He figured out what we'd need, so he got us the materials. Let's get to work," Hayden explained.

Some of the guys set up ladders while the others unloaded supplies and stacked them under the carport roof.

"I can do this, you know," Kyle told Hayden softly.

"Yeah. But now you don't have to." He handed Mitzi to Kyle. "Go on and make sure everything is being done properly. These guys are all hard workers and handy, but they aren't contractors." Hayden shooed him forward.

Two of the men were already on ladders, removing the charred boards, while others set up the saw and tables. It was like a mini construction site. These were men who were used to working together. As they talked and checked in, charred boards hit the ground and were loaded into the back of one of the trucks.

"The wood under the siding is in good shape," Dirk called. "The fire didn't reach it at all, so all the damage is superficial." That was the best news Kyle had received yet.

Kyle put Mitzi inside and Hayden joined the work crew. "What do we do with the longer boards?"

"Bring them here." Kyle powered up the saw, then cut them into small enough pieces to load on the truck. Within an hour, the old siding was off the house and the ping of nail guns pierced the evening. The saw buzzed as long pieces of siding were made level and fastened into place so they continued the lines from the adjacent walls.

Kyle got a cooler and filled it with ice and bottled water, then brought it out to the men. Basically, he checked that the work was good—and it was—he manned the saw, and he did his best to help their well-oiled machine. By the time the sun was setting, the wall had been covered and a stack of pizzas was delivered.

"Thank you all."

Dirk shrugged. "It was a pretty simple job." They all looked up at the wall of fresh wood, which would need to age a little before it was painted.

"What do I owe all of you?" Kyle asked Dirk.

"Hayden took care of the supplies. If you want to make a donation to the station, we'll use the money to purchase new equipment." Dirk patted Kyle on the shoulder. "Firefighters stick together."

Kyle swallowed. "But I'm not one of you."

Dirk turned to Hayden, who had been talking to Lee but was now watching Kyle with blazing heat in his eyes.

"I think I see." And he did. This thing with Hayden, which had started as a matter of convenience, had turned into something else, and Kyle wasn't alone in the shift in feelings. As Hayden returned his attention to the guys around him, Kyle wondered just what all this meant.

Things between them had shifted and had been moving fast. Maybe it was all too quick. Just weeks ago, Kyle was the person Hayden hated most in the world. Now Kyle had feelings for Hayden, and it seemed they were returned. Maybe this was all just a screwed-up mess, and once Hayden returned home, things would cool off between them.

Or maybe this was just a proximity thing. They had been together a lot—two healthy gay men under the same roof. Lord knows Hayden was sexy as all hell. Could it be just that?

Kyle found himself watching Hayden and knew that for him, it was more. Hayden was a good man with a kind heart. He'd done so much to help Kyle, today and for the entire time he'd been there. Hayden could have stayed in the house and in his room, keeping to himself. But he hadn't. He'd looked out for Kyle in so many ways.

The truth was that Kyle wasn't sure of Hayden's true feelings, and he was afraid of being hurt again. Only time would tell.

"Okay, let's wrap everything up," Dirk called, and the guys loaded the scraps into the trucks and packed away the ladders and tools. One of them even swept the area and took care of the sawdust.

"Thank you all so much," Kyle said as he shook hands with each of the guys.

"We help our fireman brothers," one of the younger men said and then climbed into the passenger seat of a truck to wait for one of the other men. Kyle waved as they drove away, with Dirk and Lee about to get in the final vehicle.

"I appreciate this," Hayden said.

"Dirk," Kyle called and hurried over. "I forgot in all the excitement. I think I may have seen the arsonist today." He knew he was jumping to conclusions. "He met Gavin's description, and he was hanging around where I was working at George's. He didn't stick around long, and while it felt like I should have known him, I didn't."

"Okay." Dirk pulled out a notebook. "Can you give us a better description?"

"Definitely light blond hair, my height and build. Maybe thirty years old. He was in jeans and a T-shirt. Oh…." Kyle smiled. "He had a lynx tattoo on his forearm, right here." He pointed out the position on his own body. "His clothes were scruffy and old, but I suppose that doesn't mean too much." He tried to think. "Blue eyes, and I think his nose might have been broken at some point. It was a little crooked. I don't think I can add anything else. I'm pretty sure he recognized me." Kyle was about to go toward the house. "Oh, and the car he got into was dark blue, almost black, a Toyota sedan. Older. I'm sorry I didn't get the plate. I saw him as he turned the corner. I really should have thought about it."

Dirk smiled. "This is good. I'll get it to the police officer we're working with. He'll probably want to speak to you directly, but I think we may be getting closer." He got in the truck, and Kyle waved, feeling better than he had all day. The guys had largely repaired his house, Dirk hopefully had a description of the guy they were after, and maybe Kyle was seeing some light at the end of the tunnel.

"Do you really think it was him?" Hayden asked.

"I don't know. But I got this feeling. Maybe it was dumb and this guy is a stranger, but he fit the description from last night so closely, and he was watching me to the point it felt creepy. So I tried to make a note of the guy. If it's him and he knows I've seen him… then maybe that will scare him off."

Hayden shook his head. "Or make him even more desperate. Things have been happening really quickly. Something is driving this guy."

"I know. But what more can we do? George has cameras at his building, and we're here. He already failed at burning this place, so what will he try next?" Kyle felt tension rising in his belly.

"Okay. You're probably right. As much as I'd like to think I understand this guy, none of us knows what's going to happen next." Hayden guided him toward the back door. "I was going to ask, but we were all a little busy. Did you hear about your blood test?"

"Yeah. They finished the analysis, and I had the results sent to the hospital so they can compare them with my father's to see if I'm a match. Is it bad that I keep hoping they aren't and I can have a good reason to just walk away? The thought of surgery and having something removed scares the crap out of me." And to do it for a man who treated him so badly and had kept on doing it, even when he wanted something—it just drove him crazy.

"How long before you know?" Hayden asked, and Kyle hung his head.

"When I was on the phone, I spoke to the doctor in charge. He'd been given permission to speak with me. They're going to verify the results right away. And if I'm willing and I'm a compatible match, they want to do the surgery as soon as possible. It seems Dad's condition is getting worse pretty quickly."

"I see," Hayden said and hugged him close, right under the carport. "I know you'll make the right decision. No matter what."

"I wish I knew what that was." Even as he said the words, he knew that if everything came out okay with the tests, that he'd have the surgery and do what he could to save his belligerent pain-in-the-ass father's life. It was the right thing to do. His family would be pleased, but he wasn't doing it to get back in their good graces. It was just the compassionate thing to do.

Hayden held his gaze. "Look, I'm going to tell you this. Whatever decision you make, you're going to have to live with it for the rest of your life. If you help him and regret it later… or if you need the kidney and it isn't available because you gave it away…."

Kyle nodded. That he had thought about.

"From what you told me, your father's health isn't the greatest, so even with your kidney, he may not live for very much longer. If the tests come back as compatible, then I suggest you sit down with your father and his doctor and get the real information about what difference this is going to make for you and for him. I'd also make an appointment with a transplant specialist to get information on your long-term health prospects. I know your family is looking at this as a way to prolong your father's life, but what if it shortens yours?" Hayden said. "I don't think I could stand that."

"I know. That's part of what I've been thinking about ever since he asked me. But you have good ideas, and I'm going to do that. I'll call my doctor's office in the morning and make an appointment so I can get a referral for a consultation. Because you're right. I need more information."

"Good." Hayden ran his fingers down Kyle's cheeks. "I'm not going to tell you what you should do, but I am going to say this. You have to make a well-informed decision. And if you decide to do this and have the surgery, I'll take time off work to stay home with you so you have the support you need. Your family should be good enough to do that… but I'm going to stand by whatever decision you make. You aren't going to have to go through this alone."

Kyle closed his eyes and wrapped his arms around Hayden. He had been afraid of that exact thing. If he did this, once it was over and his father had what he needed, everything would go back to the way it had been. Fuck, part of him kept wondering why he was even considering this. He'd been treated badly, and maybe since they turned their backs on him, he should do the same and have it over with. But the truth was that maybe, under it all, he was a better person than any of them. He had a conscience, even if it had taken time for him to discover it.

"Thank you." He held Hayden's gaze. "What did I ever do to deserve this kind of care?"

Hayden shrugged. "Maybe we shouldn't have to do anything. I believe that this kind of care and compassion should be what everyone receives from the people who care for them." Hayden held his gaze as Kyle swallowed hard. "Maybe it's just what we all deserve." Hayden kissed him, and Kyle slipped his arm around his neck before resting his head on his shoulder.

"I never thought I really deserved to be treated this way. My parents threw me aside, and for a long time I either felt like I wasn't good enough or right enough to be treated like this, or that I had done too many bad things in my life to be worthy of it." Kyle sighed softly. "And here I am, standing outside for all the world to see… and it's one of the people I hurt all those years ago who showed me that I was worthy to be cared for."

Hayden lightly patted the back of Kyle's head. "You're more than cared for. You have someone in your life who has come to see your heart. And it's good and worthy of being loved." He kissed him so gently that when Kyle closed his eyes, he wasn't sure if there had been a kiss at all.

"What are you saying?" Kyle asked, almost afraid to pose the question in case he got an answer he didn't like.

"What do you think? I arranged for the guys to come here and help repair your house. I'll stand by you if you decide to help your dad and give him a kidney. I've watched over you for weeks just to keep you safe. Do you think I do this for everyone in my life?" Hayden's tone was confusing, and Kyle thought he might be angry with him.

"I don't know." He didn't pull away, so that was something. "But there are times when we all just need to hear the words. I mean, I assumed that you didn't go to bed with every one of the people you rescued from burning buildings, but…."

Hayden rolled his eyes. "From my experience, words are cheap, and actions speak much louder. I try to show how I feel." He seemed hurt that Kyle hadn't understood his meaning.

"I guess I'm not used to having people care all that much." It was probably sad, but it was a fact of his life that he had come to accept.

"Then I'll say it, though a carport isn't the most romantic location. I've come to love you, Kyle. It's as strange for me as it is for you. Just a few weeks ago I thought I hated you. But that was just residual crap from school. You're a different person now, and you've shown that to me, to Mitzi, and to others, including George. They all see it, and once I let go of my old issues, I was able to see it too. I do things for you to show you how I feel. My parents, while good people, were never very openly affectionate, so I learned to judge their actions, and I guess that was how I came to show how I feel."

Kyle nodded slowly. "I think that before we get to any more of this showing, we should probably go inside so we aren't displaying everything to the neighbors." He stepped back and took Hayden's hand, then led him inside.

Mitzi was waiting for them, perched on the back of one of the living room chairs, tail wagging to beat the band. She jumped down and bounded over like she was expecting a treat.

"Did you protect the house while we were outside?" Kyle asked and gave her a bit of kibble. She looked up at him with those huge eyes, tilting her head slightly to the side. He knew she was asking for more, and Kyle lifted her into his arms. "You're my sweet girl, aren't you?"

And just like that Kyle stopped, because Mitzi wasn't his dog. She was Hayden's. Once his apartment was ready, Hayden and Mitzi would probably be leaving, and Kyle would once again be all alone. Hayden said he loved him and Kyle knew he felt the same. But things change all the time and it was hard for him to just accept. Jesus, that idea hit him harder than it should. That had always been the plan. Kyle set Mitzi down, and she ran over to Hayden for more attention.

"She's such a good girl," Hayden said as he cradled her. "I can't believe someone would just let her go." She licked his chin as he petted her.

"Me too," Kyle agreed. "But people do selfish and cruel things to hurt one another and for all sorts of other reasons."

Hayden nodded, just standing there. "I don't know about you, but I think it's time for bed. I know we've both had a very full day." He watched Kyle over Mitzi's head. "And I think it's time that we got settled in for the night."

Kyle had had enough pizza and plenty to drink, so he locked the doors and turned out most of the inside lights. He left one on downstairs before going up to his bedroom. Mitzi zoomed up past him and was on the bed when he came into the room. "I know. We aren't going to forget you, little miss." He went to the bathroom and cleaned up before undressing. Hayden wasn't up by the time he climbed under the covers and turned out the light.

Mitzi stood on the bed, watching the door. "I know, you're waiting for him too." He patted the bed, and she settled down with a soft huff, like she was exasperated. Soon enough, Hayden's footsteps sounded on the stairs.

"Are you still awake?" Hayden whispered.

Kyle sat up, and Hayden came into the room. "Of course I am. I don't fall to sleep in three minutes. What took you so long?"

"I was checking outside just to make sure we don't have a repeat of last night. Dirk told me that the police will be patrolling the area tonight and that some of the guys will be passing by as well to make sure all stays quiet. Everyone wants this to be over, and they're all doing what they can to make it happen." Hayden went to the bathroom, and afterward he turned out the lights before joining Kyle under the covers, his warm body pressing to Kyle's. "It's going to be all right. There are too many people looking into this for him to elude us for very long."

Kyle sighed. "What worries me is what he'll do before he gets caught." He rolled over, and Hayden pulled him near, pressing right to him. Kyle moaned softly, and Mitzi sighed and jumped off the bed and up onto the chair in the corner.

"I guess the dog knows the signs already," Hayden whispered.

"She's a smart one," Kyle answered and closed his eyes. In the dark room, there was nothing to see, and with his eyes shut, he could concentrate on Hayden. Or at least he tried. But he had so many things on his mind that he couldn't think straight. "I'm sorry," he whispered.

"It's okay." Hayden stopped his movements, hands stilling, and they lay quietly. "We don't have to do anything other than lie here for a while." They settled in the bed, and Mitzi returned, prancing to make her space before lying down with a "finally" sort of sigh.

CHAPTER 13

DAMN, IT had been a rough night. Kyle tossed and turned for much of it. Not that Hayden could blame him, but they seemed to take turns waking each other up. Mitzi stayed quiet all night, which hopefully meant they hadn't had any visitors.

When Kyle had finally gotten to sleep, Hayden slipped out of bed and went to the room he was using. He dressed and went downstairs. Mitzi followed, and he fed her before getting his things together to go to work.

Kyle was still asleep when he was ready to go. He crept upstairs, leaned over the bed, and lightly kissed Kyle's cheek before leaving the house.

He made it to the station just as an alarm went off. He threw the truck in Park, grabbed his gear, and jumped onto the truck as it pulled out. He changed as they rode.

"House fire to the west of town. It's bad," the captain told him. "Already called in the other company. Told the house is fully involved."

Hayden nodded and pulled on his boots and then his coat. He closed it as they drew closer to a pillar of smoke. Flames leaped toward the sky where part of the roof had been, the fire roaring in his ears. "Is anyone inside?" Hayden asked the people across the street, who pointed to where three people stood on the lawn before being moved farther back.

"Where is Jason?" Hayden asked.

"Off today. Why?" the captain asked.

"Because that's his family." Hayden immediately recognized Kyle's father standing between what had to be his wife and Kyle's sister. Holy crap.

"I'll get someone on the phone to him," the captain said, but Hayden barely heard.

"Is anyone else inside?" Hayden asked as he approached the family. He searched all three faces, hoping someone could answer. "Are you Bella?" Hayden asked, and she nodded. "Is everyone out?"

"The dog was still in there, and I don't know where he is." She was clearly in wide-eyed shock, as were all three of them.

"Let's get some medical assistance here," Hayden told the captain. "They're in shock, and Mr. Wilson is on dialysis and may need help." The captain nodded and called it in while Hayden grabbed a hose and started pouring water on what was left of the structure.

The last of the roof caved in, sending up a flood of sparks. Hoses had already wet the nearby structures, and all the hose men converged their streams into the center of what remained, sending up clouds of steam. At that point, the flames didn't last much longer and really started to die.

One of the younger guys came up and took Hayden's hose, so Hayden made his way through the neighbor's yard to the back of the house and out to the detached garage. He found the door open and went inside. The structure was intact and seemed fine. "There you are," Hayden said quietly. He took off his hat as a medium-sized black lab looked back at him, fear in her eyes. "I don't know your name, but your family is worried about you." She was an old dog with a white muzzle. The poor thing let Hayden scoop her up, and he carried her back around.

"Thank God," Kyle's mother said. She broke into tears as she saw Hayden approach with the dog. Hayden set her down, and she hurried over to the family. They petted her, and seeing the dog seemed to break through some of the shock.

"How did you know who I was? Or about Dad?" Bella asked as an EMT led her father to the newly arrived ambulance.

"I'm a friend of your brother's, and I met your father a little while ago." He refrained from explaining the details around that terrible meeting. "It looks like he's being looked after. How is your mother?"

"Shocked as hell. All of a sudden the smoke detectors went off everywhere in the house and we knew to get out. Jason's a firefighter, but he's off for a few days. He went camping with some friends."

Hayden nodded. "I've worked with him a few times. Do you have any idea where the fire started?" he asked.

"In the back toward the kitchen, I'd guess," Bella answered. "I'm not really sure. Once the smoke alarms went off, I got Mom and Dad and we made it out of the house. Then I called 911, and everything happened so fast from there. The house went up quickly. Oh God, if we'd stayed inside for much longer...." Tears welled in her eyes.

"I understand. The important thing is that everyone got out, and so did the dog." He tried to reassure her, leaving Bella to see to her mother and father.

He didn't expect to find Dirk because of the shifts he seemed to be working lately, but Lee was with his department, and Hayden approached him. "Hey, man."

"Bad one, huh?" Lee said.

"It went up fast. Real fast," Hayden told him. "And that's Kyle's family right over there."

"Got it," Lee said. "I'll make sure Dirk knows." He went back to work, and Hayden joined the guys checking that the fire was out and then helped put equipment away. He also spoke to the captain to relay his suspicions, and he agreed to work with Dirk.

"You really think this is related to all the other incidents?" Greg asked.

"I do. It's Kyle's family, and he's been the object of all the other incidents so far. His worksites on multiple occasions, his home, and now the house his family lives in goes up in flames. It's too coincidental, especially after the last few days." Hayden wished he had thought to have someone work the crowd to see if anyone was hanging around, but he'd gone into work mode and had been too busy. "I don't have any direct proof of arson, but we should look at this pretty closely."

A cry of pain went up, and Hayden hurried over toward the ambulance, where they were loading Kyle's father into the back. He was pale. Kyle's mother got in as well, and soon they headed off.

Hayden messaged Kyle and asked him to call. When he did, Hayden explained what had happened and that his parents had gone to the hospital. "Your dad wasn't doing well at all."

"Okay. Do you want me to come there?" Kyle asked.

"Your sister is all alone. Apparently your brother is out camping during his time off, so maybe this would be a good chance for you and your sister to make some sort of peace." God, he needed to stop sticking his nose where it didn't belong.

"I'll be right over," Kyle said, and Hayden hung up and got back to draining and rolling up the hoses. Everything had to be put back in just the right place so that it could be easily retrieved the next time they needed it. That took a little time but was worth it in the end.

"Kyle," Hayden called as they were finishing up. "She's over there."

Kyle nodded and hurried to where his sister waited with the dog. Hayden watched long enough to see Bella hug Kyle hard, and then he knew that maybe, at least between the two of them, things might be okay.

"Let's get back to the station so we can be ready for the next one," Greg called, and they finished up and got on the truck, a lot more tired than they had been going out. Hayden wished he could stay and be there for Kyle, because he was pretty sure he was leaving him in a tough situation, but he had a job to do, and there was little he could do to help. Hayden sat in the jump seat, wondering what the hell it would take to catch this asshole.

"YOU HAVE a couple of visitors," Greg said that afternoon as he went into his office. "Good luck." He closed the door.

Hayden wondered what was going on. He went out front. Dirk was waiting for him, with Jason right behind under a clear head of steam.

Obviously seeing Jason's mood, Dirk hung back and out of the way.

"What the hell is going on between you and my pissant little brother?" Jason demanded.

"None of your business," Hayden answered levelly. "I don't owe you an explanation for anything, and neither does Kyle." He crossed his arms over his chest. "How is your father?"

Jason growled. "No good. The little shit has dragged his feet, and now Dad's condition is too delicate and they aren't able to operate for fear it will kill him."

"I see," Hayden said gently. "So he's no longer a candidate for transplant?" That was interesting. "Was it the stress of the day that sent him over the edge, or has this been coming on?" Hayden was willing to bet that the family had waited too long to approach Kyle, and now Jason was trying to blame him for his father's deteriorating condition.

"We don't know," Jason admitted.

"Then why blame your brother? He was willing to have the tests." Hayden drew closer. "If this is how all of you act, I wouldn't blame him if he told you to go fuck yourselves sideways. I sure as hell would. But it seems he's better than that. Why, I don't know." He glared at the much bigger man, knowing Dirk was there to back him up. "What do you want? I'm assuming you came back from your camping trip for something other than to act like an ass."

"Was the fire arson?" Jason finally asked. "I know the signs. Both Mom and Bella said that the house went up really fast."

"It did, and the fire was hot," Dirk put in. "We're investigating, which is why I'm here. So go on home, and we'll be in touch with your family once we have some conclusions."

Jason clearly didn't like that answer. "I understand that Kyle has had quite a bit of unwanted attention lately. Is he the reason my family is homeless?"

"No," Dirk snapped. "If someone did burn the house, then the fault lies with the arsonist and no one else. You know that, so get these ridiculous schoolyard notions out of your thick head. If this fire was intentionally set, then there is only one person responsible, and that's the one who lit the match. You need to go so we can get on with our work. I suggest you go see your father in the hospital."

Hayden wasn't ready to let Jason go. "Have you had this little conversation with your brother?" he demanded, his belly doing flips.

"I don't need your permission to speak to Kyle."

Hayden snorted. "I'd have thought you would need your daddy's permission for something like that. From what I've heard, you do whatever Daddy wants." He loved the way Jason's head snapped back around. "Have you talked to your brother?" Hayden asked more slowly, enunciating each word.

"Not yet."

"Then go up to the hospital, and leave him alone. He doesn't need your crap, and I'm sure your father isn't going to need that drama around him either," Dirk interjected. "We have work to do, and I'm sure there are more important things that you should be doing." Dirk led the way out of the station, and Hayden followed him, leaving Jason behind. "Your captain knows where we're going."

"Good, because being around that guy gets my blood boiling." He paused just outside Dirk's truck. "I never did like him, but I always thought it was because he was Kyle's brother. You know—like I hated one, so I felt the same about the other? But no. I think I disliked him in his own right."

"Jason Wilson has always been an ass. I asked my chief not to invite him to work with us any longer. He's got a loud mouth, and he causes trouble." He had a job to do, and he had to keep his wits about him.

HAYDEN PULLED into the driveway. Kyle wasn't home yet, which wasn't surprising. He'd been working hard. Hayden walked around the house to check that everything was okay before going inside. He got the leash and took Mitzi for a walk right away so she could do her business.

He was really coming to love this little dog, just like he was growing to love Kyle. He'd thought about his evolving feelings a lot over the past few days and had decided to chalk them up to a "truth is stranger than fiction" kind of thing. Hayden wasn't the same person he'd been in school. He was more confident now. Kyle wasn't the same either. It seemed that for Kyle, life had thrown him a number of curveballs and had beaten him down.

Mitzi tugged Hayden over toward a tree, and he let her sniff and explore. She finished her business, and Hayden used a bag to pick up her poo. Then she turned back toward the house like she was done and ready to go home. "Okay, little girl, let's head on home, then." He walked her back, and just before they reached the house, Kyle turned into the drive, the truck almost screeching to a halt. Kyle climbed out and slammed the door behind him.

Both Hayden and Mitzi started, and she pulled away, barking sharply. "What happened?" Hayden could only guess. "Jason?"

The force Kyle used to whip around to him was so sharp, Hayden could almost physically feel it. "How did you know?"

"He came to the station today demanding answers and sticking his nose into things that don't concern him. How's your dad?" Hayden asked, changing the subject. "Your brother said that he wasn't doing well. It was about the only thing that Dirk and I got out of him that wasn't a spewed pile of crap."

Kyle shrugged. "I went to the hospital to see him and to try to get some information from Mom, but Jason kept me away. Bella was pissed, and she came to find me. Dad isn't well at all and is too weak for any surgery. They are trying to get him stronger and doing more dialysis. But the thing is… the tests came back, and I'm only a partial match. Which means they could use my kidney, but there would be a greater chance of rejection, and with my father so weak, they aren't going to chance it. The risks to both of us are too great."

"So they'll do nothing?" Hayden asked as Kyle squatted down and Mitzi practically bounded into his arms.

"Basically, I'm off the hook as a donor, though apparently Jason blames me for that. He says I should have agreed faster, and maybe then I could have helped Dad. But I doubt it, with Dad in this kind of shape, and I wasn't a really good match anyway."

Hayden nodded. "It wasn't going to help, and would only put you in danger."

"Yeah. I don't know how my mother feels. Jason is angry, but that's on him, and he isn't likely to see reason. All he wants is whatever Dad wants, and he's mad and pretty useless at the moment. He was never very clearheaded." At least some of Kyle's frustration had slipped away.

"Come on. Let's go inside," Hayden said, and Kyle carried Mitzi into the house. As soon as Kyle set her down, she explored her food and water bowls before trotting away through the house.

"How bad was it at Mom and Dad's?" Kyle asked.

"I'm afraid it's pretty much a total loss. The fire was hot enough that it burned through the carpet and subfloor, which means that the heat got into the basement as well, so there wasn't a great deal left inside."

Kyle hung his head. "That's going to kill Mom. All her pictures and the things she collected over the years are probably all gone."

Hayden nodded. He knew the cost that a house fire could take. It wiped out family histories, and they often could never be rebuilt. It wasn't the furniture or the clothes that were the real loss, but the irreplaceable things that no amount of money could ever make up for.

"I'll have to wait and see what happens next. I suspect that now that they don't have much need for me,

I'll return to being someone they'll continue their lives without." He shrugged, and Hayden knew Kyle was trying to slough it off, but it seemed to hurt him, the pain clear in his eyes.

Hayden could have said something trite or expected. Instead, he wrapped his arms around Kyle and said nothing. There was little he could do other than be there, and maybe that was the most important thing. The rest would take care of itself. At least he hoped.

"I suppose I'm not worse off than I was before. But I would have thought that my willingness to help would count for something." He buried his head against Hayden's shoulder.

Hayden held Kyle a little tighter and gave him the privacy of his own thoughts and feelings. "It's not your fault."

"I know, but it still hurts," Kyle said. They stood together quietly, only the sound of the refrigerator compressor from the other room breaking the quiet. "What do I do now?"

Hayden shrugged. "If you ask me, I'd say nothing. The ball is in their court. If they make an overture, then you need to decide how you want to respond. But for now, it's up to them." He wished to hell that Kyle could have a little peace. "If you want, I was thinking that we could walk downtown and maybe get something to eat. Get out of the house. It's a nice evening, and some fresh air might help."

"I don't know if anything is going to help. Or if I'm worth all this." Kyle blinked as he pulled away. "Maybe you should just go on your way too. I'm clearly not worth bothering with." Shoulders slumped, Kyle left the room.

"Really?" Hayden called after him. "You're going to stand there being sorry for yourself? Maybe you're entitled and maybe you aren't. But is that what you're really going to do?" Hayden shook his head.

"I'm being realistic."

"Fatalistic is more like it," Hayden countered. "There's no reason for it, and you know damned well that isn't going to help anyone at all. You can act that way all you like, but it isn't going to change anything. So your father is an ass and your brother is a dick. I saw you and your sister. If a renewed relationship with her is all you get out of this, you're still ahead if you ask me." He sat in one of the chairs and put his feet up on the stool. Mitzi jumped into his lap, and he petted her gently.

Kyle had to come to his own conclusions, and even if Hayden thought he was doing the wrong thing, they were his feelings and he had to work through them on his own.

"Maybe you're right," Kyle said as he returned.

Hayden smiled. "Of course I am. I've never hesitated to admit when I'm wrong. Thankfully it doesn't happen all that often—"

"Ass," Kyle snapped and sat on the end of the sofa closest to him.

Hayden grinned. "I've been called that before."

"I bet you have… and I've been called worse," Kyle added. "By my brother, in fact."

Hayden leaned forward. "We can't control what others think of us. All we have control over is how we see ourselves." God, that sounded incredibly profound, and Hayden wondered if he had heard it somewhere else. He must have, because he wasn't in the habit of deep thinking.

"That's true, I guess," Kyle said. "But I think we have more pressing things. Like getting ourselves some dinner before our stomachs eat themselves." He got up, and Hayden followed.

Hayden fed Mitzi and got her settled with a treat, and then they left the house. Hayden made sure everything was closed up tight, and started toward town.

It was a beautiful summer evening. "I can almost forget all the shit that happened on a night like this." The breeze was perfect, and trees rustled overhead. The courthouse bell chimed the seven o'clock hour.

Kyle's phone rang, and he answered it. "Hey, Bella." Hayden breathed a sigh of relief. "That's good. At least he's out of immediate danger." Kyle listened as they continued walking. "So all they can do is continue treatment and hope he'll get stronger?" Somehow Hayden figured that was wishful thinking. Dialysis took a lot out of a person, physically and emotionally. "Yeah… of course. What about the insurance company? Have they said anything?" He listened for a while longer, making small gestures of understanding but not saying very much. "Okay. I know a good realtor. She helped me find my house, and I'm sure she can help you and Mom find temporary housing… or a new home, if that's what she wants." He grew quiet once more. "I'll text it over." Kyle talked for a few more minutes and then ended the call.

"That sounded promising."

Kyle half smiled and nodded. "I think it was. The insurance company is getting Mom some money, and Bella says that Mom wants a new house." He sent a text and then shoved his phone in his pocket. "She said she was sorry for how she acted and that she was wrong to listen to Dad like that."

"How is the old goat?" Hayden asked.

"Hanging on. They're hopeful, but I don't know how realistic it is. Still, he seems to be fighting, so that's good. Bella said that Mom would like to meet me for lunch so we can talk." The hope in Kyle's voice was positive, but Hayden prayed to hell they didn't leave him hanging again.

"Do you want me to go with you?" Hayden asked.

Kyle stopped walking. "Would you? I don't know what I have to say to her. There's still so much hurt, and if there is a chance for healing, I don't want to blow it…."

Hayden rested his hand on Kyle's shoulder. "You won't. But as long as I can get away, I'll go with you."

Kyle nodded. "Does it seem strange to you how well things are going between us?" He started walking once again. "I mean… it's like I found the one person who understands me and seems to get what I need." He swung his arms a little like a happy kid. "And you listen."

Hayden shrugged. "I don't know quite what to make of it either. I guess I'm taking things as they come, and I'm grateful for it."

They continued walking without talking until they reached the main intersection of town. "Do you believe in destiny or fate?" Kyle was certainly filled with unexpected questions tonight.

"I don't know. Not really. If there is such a thing as destiny, then I believe we make our own. I think our lives are made up of the decisions we make. Back in high school, you made decisions, and so did I. Good or bad, we made them. Years later, we made different ones, and it was those that brought us here." He thought for a few seconds. "On the whole, I don't think

I'd change anything." He reached for Kyle and took his hand. "The things we decided brought us together. It may not have been a very straight or easy path, but we're here. And maybe we can just be happy about it." He squeezed Kyle's fingers and then let go because of where they were. Carlisle was a good town and pretty safe, but there was no use drawing attention. "I mean, we could question everything, chew on each decision and fork in the road until we take all the fun out of life. Maybe destiny is just recognizing the good stuff when it comes your way."

"Maybe," Kyle agreed. "But you're really getting deep again. And maybe that's something I need to do more. Not that I'm grateful that some arsonist is after the places I work and tried to burn down my house or set fire to my folks' place, but maybe he brought me back part of my family, and I can be thankful for at least that little piece."

"Hayden!" a voice called over the traffic. Hayden turned and heard it again. "Hayden!"

"George?" Hayden said as George hurried toward them. "What's wrong?" They were about to cross to the west, but instead they moved north toward where George waited.

"I was just coming to direct the police and stuff. I think there's someone in the building. I called the police and the fire department. The cameras picked up movement." George turned, and they followed him to Hayden's building.

Hayden phoned the station directly and found out that a truck was already on the way. He hurried up to the door at the base of the stairs and pounded on it, making a hell of a lot of noise. There was a fire escape in the back. Maybe if someone was inside, they would get scared and duck out. The important thing was to keep the building from going up in smoke.

"Should we go inside?" Kyle asked.

"Be careful. If he is in there, then he could be armed, and I'm not prepared to handle a standoff." Hayden pounded on the door once more before opening it and stomping up the first few stairs. He didn't go any farther and stepped back out again as the first police officers arrived.

"Hey, Red, Carter," Hayden called. "No one is supposed to be inside, and George, the owner, saw movement on one of the cameras. Someone tried to set the building on fire a few days ago, so it's possible our arsonist is back." He figured he should tell them all they knew and suspected.

"Have you been inside?" Red asked.

"Just up the first few stairs. I was hoping to scare him off before he set the place ablaze." Hayden stepped back just as an explosion rocked him to the ground. He managed to get up and raced away from the building, pulling George and Kyle back along the sidewalk as the upper floor burst into a fireball. Red and Carter pulled back as well. "Is everyone okay?" Hayden called as fire trucks pulled up in front.

Hayden explained what happened to the chief and checked on George and Kyle, who were okay for the most part. George had a cut on his cheek, probably from broken glass. Red called for an ambulance as Hayden administered first aid from the department kit. Kyle stood nearby, and every time Hayden chanced a glance at George, he was watching the top of the building burn.

"Don't even think it," Hayden told him with a glare.

"Think what?" George asked with a wince as Hayden applied pressure to the cut.

"That this was his fault," Hayden answered.

"Fuck no. It sure as hell isn't. If I get my hands on this guy, I'm going to rip his ears off and shove them down his throat."

Hayden smiled at his colorful language. "We'll have to see about that."

The teams of firefighters fought the blaze, bringing it under control fairly quickly.

"It looks like it was concentrated in the front, and much of the force went out that way," Dirk told them just as the ambulance arrived. "That's good, because maybe the buildings on either side won't be as damaged." It was still going to be a real mess for a lot of people.

"Make sure the fire doesn't spread. I can fix the damned building, but there are plenty of people who live in the places on both sides," George said.

"We're going unit by unit to make sure everyone is out, and the Red Cross is already here helping folks," Dirk told George. "Everything is being handled. Do you want us to call someone for you?"

"I already did. My wife is on her way, and she's going to be a right terror when she sees this mess." George lay back as the paramedics checked him over and got him bandaged.

Hayden went to locate Kyle and found him a ways down the block, leaning against one of the buildings, pale as a ghost.

"Is this ever going to end?" he asked before slumping to the sidewalk.

CHAPTER 14

KYLE SAT where he was, unable to move. All he could think about was how Hayden had now lost his home. The building was gone, the top floor blown out. What next? George had been right, and someone had been inside. Maybe if they were lucky, the idiot had gotten caught inside and had blown himself to hell along with the building. Not that Kyle had that kind of luck, but a guy could hope.

"Kyle," Hayden whispered as he pressed something cold and wet into his hand. "Drink some water."

Kyle managed to lift his gaze from the weathered gray concrete and took a drink, the cool liquid sliding down his throat. "Is everyone okay?"

"Yes. George is with the EMTs. They're bandaging him up, and he's flirting with one of them. The fire is nearly out, and as far as they can tell, everyone is out of the nearby buildings and accounted for."

At least that was a blessing. It was probably a miracle that no one had been hurt.

A crash echoed down the street, and Kyle looked up as everyone scrambled away, pieces of the building façade falling to the ground. The firefighters continued pouring water on the building from a greater distance, more smoke and steam rising from the gaping second-floor hole. "Did they find anyone?"

"The police are checking in back," Hayden answered. "Drink some more water."

Kyle did as he was told without thinking about it. "I have to do something to stop this."

Hayden helped him to his feet. "There's nothing either of us can do. This guy has his own agenda, and God knows what he'll do next. He's already broken in here twice, and I dare say he either set the fire and got caught in it, or rigged the place to explode once he was outside. Either way, this is more than just setting a fire."

Kyle understood that. The arsonist was escalating, and it was happening fast. This guy was becoming more and more desperate, and getting closer to Kyle all the damned time. His family's home, the building where he was working…. The only place still standing was his house, and Kyle wondered how long that would last. "We need to get home," Kyle said. "Now."

Hayden nodded, and after talking to the chief, he spoke with Red, who got them into the patrol car with Carter and took off toward Kyle's house. Red parked in the drive, and Kyle handed him his house keys. Red unlocked the door and went inside, followed by Carter. They left the door open. Kyle watched as they opened windows before coming out.

"The gas was on in the kitchen. I shut it off and opened things up. Give it a few minutes." Red inhaled deeply, his eyes watering.

"What about the dog?" Kyle asked as panic rose inside him. He got out of the car and hurried toward the door, but Hayden grabbed him and pulled him to a stop.

"We need to wait. The door is open, and the house needs to air out a few more minutes," Hayden cautioned, holding him closer while Kyle kept watching the front door, willing Mitzi to come racing out. But that didn't happen, and with each passing second, he grew more tense.

"Let's go see what's going on," Red said. "The gas should have dissipated by now." He took the lead, checking out the interior of the house before allowing them inside.

The scent of gas lingered, but the air was pretty clear. Kyle raced upstairs, where he checked each room and even the closets for the dog. But she was nowhere to be found. "Hayden," he said as he came back downstairs, "do you think she got out?"

"Either that or he took her," Hayden offered and pulled out his phone. "When I took Mitzi to the vet to have her looked at, Mitchell suggested that since she was a stray, she might try to return to a previous home, so we chipped her and put a GPS tracker on her the same color as her collar." He showed the screen to Red. "It looks like she's moving fast."

"Definitely in a car," Red told them and called in their suspicion. "I need to follow this."

"Then we're coming with you," Kyle said as he got back in the police cruiser. "Are you two coming, or are we just going to waste time?" He was ready to get Mitzi back and bring all of this to an end. He closed the door, glaring at the others until Red and Carter shrugged and got in the car.

"Stay inside the car no matter what happens," Carter instructed as Red skirted the center of town, heading west on South Street before maneuvering to High Street.

"The dog is probably a couple miles ahead and has stopped moving." Hayden showed Kyle the display. "I think he's on Newville Road."

Red made the cut over, and they continued on, drawing closer to where the app said Mitzi was. Red doused the siren as they drew up to a white house with a well-kept yard, a dark blue Toyota in the driveway.

"That's the car I saw outside George's building after work the other day," Kyle said as Red pulled to a stop.

"Call it in," Red said. "We're going to need backup. Who knows what this guy is capable of?" He parked on the street while Carter called for reinforcements. "It's state police jurisdiction out here."

Hayden made another call while Kyle chewed his nails and wished things would happen faster.

A bark from inside and a dash of brown hair caught his attention, and then Mitzi burst out from around the side of the garage, racing their way. "Open the door," Red said.

Carter cracked his.

"Mitzi!" Kyle called, and she jumped into the police car and pranced over Carter until she peered through the mesh into the back seat, tail wagging, excited doggie bliss in her eyes.

"You're such a good girl," Kyle crooned, smiling at her until Carter gently lifted her and brought her to the back, opened the door, and set Mitzi in Kyle's lap. She bounded around both of them, getting pets and licking their fingers.

"How did you get out?" Hayden asked as sirens sounded in the distance. Kyle checked Mitzi over to make sure she wasn't hurt. "Red, there's something attached to her collar."

"Don't touch it," Carter said, staying on the far side of the car. He pulled on gloves and opened the back door, staying low. After taking the small container, he checked it over before opening it and carefully pulling out a small note.

"Suicide note?" Red asked.

"Yeah. Basically he's threatening to blow up the house and himself if anyone comes too close," Carter said. He called in an update as more police vehicles arrived. Local police, troopers, fire trucks—everything converged on the small house.

Red and Carter joined the rest of the officers while Kyle sat in the back of the car with Hayden and Mitzi. Police officers took up positions around the house, pinning the guy down and setting up a post to speak to him. The activity was fascinating, but all Kyle wanted to do was go home. He had Hayden and Mitzi, everything important. The rest he didn't need to see.

Carter opened the back door to poke his head inside. "He wants to talk to you," Carter told Kyle.

"Me?" he asked.

"Yes. He's asked to speak to you by name. He knows you're here. The plates have been run, and we have a name—Richard Burke. Does that ring a bell for either of you?" Carter asked.

Hayden gasped. "I know him. Dick and I were in the same homeroom together. I think we may have had gym class together or something." He turned to Kyle, who shrugged.

"I remember the guy, but we didn't hang in the same circles." Kyle tried to recall if he had picked on the guy, but nothing came to mind. "He was one of those people who stayed on the sidelines. He was there but not there, I guess." Kyle searched his memory to try to think if he had had anything to do with him at all.

"Did you pick on him?" Hayden asked, and Kyle shrugged.

"I remember Dickie Burke. We were in middle school and high school together, but I don't think I ever paid any attention to him. Did you?" Kyle asked. "He was like the wallpaper or something."

"Will you talk to him?" Carter asked.

"I guess." If nothing else, maybe Kyle could get some answers about what had been going on. As it was, he had no clue as to why any of this had happened. "I don't know what he wants or what I can do to help."

"Just talk to him, or better yet, let him do the talking. Don't try to get him to tell you anything or put pressure on him. We're trying to figure out where he is in the house. Everything will be recorded, so…."

Kyle nodded and followed Carter to one of the other cars.

"Richard, it's me, Kyle," he said into the phone they pressed into his hand. "You wanted to talk to me." He had no idea what else to say. He waited for a few seconds. "Are you there?" He waited once again.

"You are there." His voice sounded rough. "Did you like my messages? I've been sending them for months."

Kyle looked at Carter, who motioned for him to keep talking.

"I don't understand what you're trying to tell me." He didn't get fucking anything. Why would a guy he barely remembered want to burn down every place Kyle was associated with? "Why do all this?"

"Nope, nope. It isn't that easy," he said. "This isn't some stupid movie where I'm going to tell you all my plans and shit. You're going to have to figure this one out on your own." He seemed kind of happy.

"Why? I don't know what your message is." He was tempted to say that he barely remembered the guy at all. "You've been trying to get my attention for a while now, but what good is it if I don't understand what you want?"

"*Want*…? It should be obvious what I want. I want to take away everything you have, just like you did to me."

Kyle turned to Hayden, his chest aching. He shrugged, and Carter motioned him to keep going.

"Keep him talking about himself. That helps," he said quietly.

"How did I do that?" Kyle questioned. "I know we went to high school together and that we had a few classes together. But I don't remember that I took anything from you." He tried to keep his voice level as something in the house smashed in the background.

"You don't remember? Of course you don't." Another smash, and Carter motioned once more for Kyle to keep talking.

"Then why don't you tell me?" Kyle said gently. "I'm trying, but it was a while ago."

"Not that long," Richard said, and it dawned on Kyle that he had assumed this was something related to them being in school, but maybe it was more recent. He took a deep breath and decided to try a completely different angle.

"Okay. What do you do for work?" He figured it was a general question and that it would keep him talking about something. Kyle had no idea what he was doing.

"I'm a carpenter," Richard answered.

Kyle's gaze immediately snapped to Hayden. "What kind? What's your specialty?" Kyle asked, the back of his neck tingling for a few seconds. "I always love the fine detail work that really makes a project special." He waited but received only silence. He checked that the call was still connected and saw that it seemed to be. "Are you there?"

"I am" was all he received in reply.

Kyle moved the phone away. "He's a carpenter."

"Does that ring a bell?" Hayden asked.

Kyle nodded. "I wish I had my records. I was looking for help a few years ago, and I got a number of applications. I hired someone, but he didn't work out, and I was going to try someone else, but I figured I'd just do the work myself." He had gotten quite a few résumés.

"Are you remembering?" Richard snapped.

Kyle wasn't sure what to say and went for honesty. "I don't think so. Did you apply for a position to work with me?" He was getting more confused, but the police were moving into position. He figured he needed to keep Richard occupied.

"How could you not hire me? We were friends. I applied for a job, and you never even bothered to call me back."

What the hell? Kyle could barely remember him, and somehow they had supposedly been friends? He had figured that something was wrong with Richard, but now he had proof of a sort. The guy had to be delusional.

"Keep him talking any way you can," Carter instructed. "Get him focused on you."

Kyle nodded, so he figured he might as well go for it all the way. "I don't remember you and I being friends. I saw you in the hallway, and we had a few classes together. We might have even sat across the aisle from each other. But when were we friends?"

"Junior year in English class. We studied before tests together while waiting for Mr. Mell. Remember? We'd memorize those stupid phrases and crap before the Friday tests. We did that every week."

Kyle remembered now. "Everyone did that with the people around them." It had just been a matter of convenience and a way to overcome one of the bullshit assignments. Kyle had never given it a second thought, not then or afterward. It was just something they did in school.

"But it was every week, and you were nice… at least during class," Richard said.

Kyle shook his head. Damn, here was a guy so starved for any sort of positivity that he'd made up this whole friendship based on something Kyle had never given a second thought to. Years later he actually expected Kyle to remember this friendship that never was and help him with a job? Kyle's head ached.

"Yeah, well, we were friends, and you advertised for a carpenter, and I applied. I'd have thought you would have remembered me. I needed a job, and I'm good at what I do. But I never heard from you. Like I wasn't good enough or something. I need a damn job! We went to school together, and you couldn't be bothered. I lost my house, and all I have left is my car, and they're going to take that!"

Kyle pulled the phone away from his ear.

Jesus. Kyle held Hayden's gaze, and he came closer, slipping his arm around Kyle's waist. "It's okay," Hayden mouthed.

"How was I supposed to know?" Kyle asked Richard. "You blame me for not helping you when I had no way of knowing any of this. I was just trying to hire someone, that's all."

A smash sounded once again, and this time Kyle jumped. He turned toward the house just as a chair sailed through one of the large windows. Then all hell broke loose. Police ran toward the house and went in the front door.

"Make sure everything is ready," Hayden told the firefighters. "He has a habit of setting everything on fire." Hoses stood laid out, ready to be turned on, firefighters in positions of cover in case they were needed. It was like everything held still for a minute, and then shots were fired and police officers streamed out the front door, diving in either direction just before the building went up in a huge fireball that roiled upward.

Kyle hit the ground when the shock wave reached him. It blew past, searing heat washing over him and then cooling in an instant.

"Get all the officers back here!" one of the police captains called as officers took up positions with their guns while others hurried forward to help those up near the house get away from the inferno.

"Head count!" someone yelled, and after a few seconds Kyle heard an officer report that everyone except the suspect was accounted for. "Where was he?"

The officer looked toward the burning building. "He didn't make it out." He turned away, and the captain motioned to the firefighters, who began dousing the flames. There was so little left of the building, much of it strewn over the front, back, and side yards. Smoke rose all around. The larger flames were doused before the firefighters moved closer, adding water to where someone's home had once stood.

"I'm sorry," Kyle said to the people still around him. "I had no idea."

Hayden was the first to respond. "Of course you didn't. How were you to know? This was all in his head. His problems were of his own making, but it was easier to blame them on you, someone he barely knew. He made up this entire friendship, and out of that, an obligation that you didn't fulfill."

"But—"

"No buts. This was all in his mind. A way for him to shift the blame for the way his life had gone from himself to you. And the longer he did it, the easier it was for him to believe his own stories."

Kyle heard what Hayden was saying, but it was difficult to believe. He must have missed something. "You know, I could have dealt with him being mad at me for how I acted in high school. Hell, if I'd been a dick to the guy, at least it would be a solid reason for what he did. This just seems so strange. He had this whole relationship with me in his head that I had no idea about." He handed the phone back to Carter and took a deep breath to try to clear his head. "I don't think I'll ever understand."

"Maybe not. But this isn't on you," Carter said. "Hayden is right. He fabricated a relationship that only existed in his mind, and somehow you became the object of his obsession. You were just a kid in school, and he needed a friend so badly that he made one up. And years later, when he encountered you again, even tangentially, he had this friendship that to him was real, and when you didn't respond, it sent him in a spiral." He clamped his hand on Kyle's shoulder. "I'm serious. There's no blame for you here."

Kyle nodded, trying to let that message sink in. "It's hard to accept, though. He's dead, and he destroyed so much just to try to get my attention. You know? It sucks. I was mean to Hayden in school, and look at us. Apparently I was nice to him, and look what the hell happened."

Hayden rolled his eyes. "Does that mean you're going to stop being nice to everyone in case they turn into an arsonist and try to set fire to half the town?"

Kyle groaned. "You really are an ass sometimes."

"I think we've been over that already." He smiled and hugged Kyle tight. "I think we both need to let go of our regrets and what we did in the past. That's over. We can't change it. All we can do is worry about today. We have our little girl back, and she led us to the arsonist. He isn't going to be setting any more fires."

"You're just a barrel of laughs, aren't you?" Kyle quipped. "And I agree. Let the past stay there." He could learn from it, but Kyle didn't need to live there any more than Hayden did. The two of them had a chance at a future, and that was more important than things that happened years ago.

"Red and I will take you home in a little while," Carter told them before leaving the two of them alone.

He had work to do, and Kyle just needed a little quiet at the moment, even if it was a bubble of peace in a world of chaos all around them. Kyle picked up Mitzi, the three of them together again. He wasn't sure what was to come, but he hoped to hell it involved all of them.

CHAPTER 15

SOMETIMES QUIET was a relief, but mostly it was a pain in the ass, especially when he was waiting for something. The police had taken over the scene of the explosion and had been sifting through the remains for the past few days. "Hayden, the chief wants to see you."

"Thanks," he answered without looking at who it was. Maybe now he'd get some answers or have his ass chewed out. Lord knows which was coming. Maybe both. He went to the office and knocked on the doorframe.

"Get inside and close the door," Greg said and motioned to a chair. "I should dress you down for hitching a ride after a damned dog."

Hayden narrowed his gaze. "She's my dog, and I was simply trying to get her back."

"You should have let the police handle it. Instead, you and your boyfriend got yourself in the middle of a real mess, and everyone wants answers." He sat back, and Hayden shrugged.

"We all want answers that we aren't going to get." He had spent the past two evenings talking things over with Kyle, going round and round and basically getting nowhere because sometimes there weren't any answers to be had. "No one was injured except the suspect, and in the end, he blew up his mother's home. Thankfully she wasn't there. Yes, there are messes to clean up in town, but that'll happen with time. Everyone is alive—"

"Except the suspect. I'm glad I'm not the police chief," Greg said, and Hayden just shrugged again. As far as he was concerned, Richard got what he deserved—in essence he'd killed himself with one of his own fires. That had a kind of poetic justice. "Look, they did recover a body from the remains of the house, and it checks out as Richard Burke. So at least that part of the story is over."

Hayden figured the captain had been blustering and letting off steam. "Yeah, it is. Kyle's family is getting their feet under them. His mom is looking at houses, and once the insurance company comes through, they'll buy something. George is working with his insurance company to rebuild on Hanover Street." Apparently he had decided to use Kyle as the general contractor for the job.

"There's just one more thing," Greg said and handed him a note. "Your little dog. The one who led you to the arsonist—someone has come forward saying they could be her owner. The message was passed to me through the police. Here is their contact information."

Hayden took the paper, and numbness sank in. "I see," he said softly. Damn, that had come out of left field. He had hoped that he and Kyle would be able to keep Mitzi, but if a family out there had lost her…. Word had apparently gotten through town pretty quickly about the little dog that had led to the Carlisle Arsonist, as the papers had dubbed him. There had even been a picture of her in the paper, so…. "Thanks." How the hell was he going to tell Kyle?

"HOW WAS your day?" Kyle asked from the kitchen as soon as Hayden walked in the door. Mitzi went nuts, jumping around his legs for her hello pets and attention. Hayden gave her some love, trying not to think about the possibility that this could be the last time she greeted him. "That bad?"

Hayden shrugged and wished he could skip the bad shit. Kyle seemed happy. "How did things go for you?"

"Real good. Ellen has decided to repair her place, and the work is going to start in the next few weeks. She's asked me to oversee all of it. So that's good. George has done the same, so it looks like my little home improvement business is expanding into general contracting. Mom called. She and I talked for a long while. Dad is out of the hospital and up to his usual mean behavior. Even dying, he's still an ass." Kyle grinned. "Mom told him that he needed to change his tune or else he'd find himself living alone in a hotel room somewhere. Apparently she's realized he's full of crap. She and Bella have decided they're done listening to him. I don't know how long it will last, but I'm hopeful."

"Is she actively looking at houses now?" Hayden asked, sitting at the table.

"She says she will in a few weeks once all the insurance company stuff is done. She wants to get settled. Dad wants to move into a senior living place, but Mom told him that she'd be the one looking at houses and choosing what she wanted. It was beautiful." He stirred a pot of pasta. "I never thought she had it in her."

"Just goes to show that people can surprise you." He stood and came up behind Kyle, then slipped his arms around his waist. He rested his head against Kyle's shoulder and closed his eyes.

"What's wrong?" Kyle asked, turning in his arms. "You're tense and worried. I can feel it."

Hayden held Kyle's gaze. "I got a message at the station. Someone has come forward claiming to be Mitzi's owner. The police were contacted, and they got word to the captain. I called the number from work and spoke to a man who claims that she's his." He didn't want it to be true. "He says her name is Roxy."

Kyle slumped against him. "You have to be fucking kidding me," he groaned. "Can't we just say that she ran away and keep her in the house?" He sighed. "I'm kidding… but kind of not."

"There's nothing we can do. He came through the proper channels. I called him, and he's going to be here in about an hour. I wasn't sure how you'd feel, but I thought it best to meet the guy here on our own turf."

He was starting to think of the house as home, even if they hadn't talked about it much. He and Kyle had just gone forward for the past few days, but Hayden was starting to think he might need to find another place to live.

Kyle's expression fell right before Hayden's eyes. "How can I just give her up? She's a part of the family, a part of us." He lifted Mitzi into his arms and cradled her as she licked his chin.

Hayden just held Kyle, unable to find words. This was the first time Kyle had used those words, echoing the feelings that Hayden had yet to express himself. Maybe one of the things the two of them needed to talk about was expressing themselves better. Hayden knew he needed to improve in that area, and it seemed Kyle might as well.

"What do we do?" Kyle asked.

"I don't know. We'll have to see if she acts like she knows him. I don't have any reason to suspect that he isn't the owner. But then, I don't know for sure that he is." Hayden gently took Mitzi from Kyle and set her on the floor. She hurried off, and Hayden followed her into the living room, where she curled up in her favorite chair. He left the room and returned to the kitchen.

"What are you doing?" Kyle asked.

"An experiment," Hayden answered. "Roxy," he called and waited before calling again. He hoped like hell not to hear the click of her nails on the floor. "Mitzi," he switched, and the nails clickety-clicked as she came running.

"She didn't come," Kyle said.

"Nope. Roxy," he said again. Mitzi ignored him, checking around the kitchen for goodies. "Roxy, is that your name?" he asked again and got no response. "Mitzi," he said, and she turned her head toward him before coming over to nuzzle his hand.

"Her name is definitely not Roxy," Kyle said. "So what do we do?"

Hayden hesitated before making a quick call to Red. "Need a favor. Are you and Terry busy tonight?" He turned to Kyle, who nodded.

"No. Why?"

"Wanna join us for dinner? The dog I picked up at a fire a while ago—someone has come forward claiming she's his, but Mitzi doesn't respond to the name."

"And you wanna see if this guy is on the level?" Red asked. "You think he might be up to something?"

"It's possible. I thought if you guys were here as witnesses, then if there is anything wrong...." He wasn't going to give Mitzi up unless this truly was her owner, and they were going to have to prove it.

Red and Terry talked, and then Red returned to the phone.

"Terry has to teach a lifesaving class this evening. I can drop him off and then be there in about forty-five minutes. Does that work? I can pick him up after his class."

"Perfect," Hayden agreed. "That's awesome. I really appreciate it."

"I'll see you then," Red said, and Hayden felt better. If this was Mitzi's owner, then they would have to say goodbye to the little dog who had captured both their hearts. They would have to see what happened.

"THIS IS really good," Hayden said as he finished the last of the pasta with alfredo sauce.

"I just followed the recipe I found online." Kyle stood to take care of the dishes, and Hayden took his arm.

"I'll do that. You cooked me a feast, so it's the least I can do." Hayden put the dishes in the dishwasher and was wiping down the counter as the rumble of a powerful engine drew into the drive. Kyle stilled, and Hayden stood next to him.

"I wish Red was here," Kyle whispered.

"He will be soon."

Hayden went to the back door and peered out at a truck so far off the ground that there was no way Mitzi could get out of it without hurting herself. The engine cut off, and a huge man got out of the truck and approached the door.

"Where's Roxy?" he asked, and Hayden opened the door farther to let him inside. "I'm Gene." He shook Hayden's hand. "There's my Roxy," he said, kneeling down. Mitzi approached him, sniffed him, and hurried away.

"Are you sure she's your dog?" Hayden asked. "She's always been really affectionate to both of us." He didn't like this one bit.

"Roxy was actually my sister's dog, and she ran away when Gale left," Gene told him. That sounded like a story.

"So she isn't your dog? I was told that you said she was yours." Mitzi stayed behind Hayden's legs, and Kyle picked her up. When Gene tried to pet her, she snapped at him the same way she had with Kyle's father. "She really doesn't seem to like you." Hayden was beginning to share the feeling. "Like I said, are you sure you have the right dog? We tried calling her Roxy and she ignored us. It's possible you have the wrong dog." Hayden kept trying to let the man off the hook.

A knock sounded on the back door. "I'll get it." Kyle left the room. Hayden heard the back door open and knew Red had come in.

"I'm sorry, but I can't let Mitzi go with you," Hayden said gently, keeping a smile in place.

Gene looked around the house and anywhere but at Hayden. "It's pretty clear that Roxy likes both of you," Gene said. "And you seem to care for her, so maybe we can come to an arrangement. Gale left town, and Roxy ran away. So maybe if you just buy the dog, then everything would be okay. I can send her the money and she can get herself a puppy." He stepped closer. "I think five hundred is fair. Then you'll own the dog."

This was exactly what Hayden had been afraid of.

"I have to ask, Gene. Is this really your dog or your sister's dog, or did you just see her picture in the paper and think you could get something out of it? Because this clearly isn't Roxy." He narrowed his gaze. "Are you sure you have the right dog?" he pressed, again giving the guy a way out. "Because if you're mistaken, no harm, no foul. It happens." He smiled, playing dumb.

Something about the entire situation had rubbed him the wrong way from the beginning, and as soon as he met Gene, Hayden had known something wasn't right. Just the way he refused to look Hayden square on told him a lot.

"No. I'm sure that's my sister's dog."

"And you're willing to sell her for five hundred dollars."

"I think I've heard enough," Red said, striding into the room. Gene's expression changed in an instant, growing hard and defensive. "Do you have any proof that she's your sister's dog?" Red asked. "A bill of sale? Maybe some pictures of you or her with the dog?" Red was a force of nature. "Because what I heard was attempted extortion."

"And who are you to tell me anything?"

Red glared. "Officer Redmond Markham, Carlisle Police." The way he looked was a thing of beauty, but the way Gene looked like he wanted to crawl into a hole and die was even better. "I believe that you have no claim on this dog at all. I'm also willing to bet you probably don't have a sister. This is all some scam to make a quick buck. Isn't it?"

Gene looked over his shoulder. "I think I'm going to go now."

"I think that's a good idea. You need to leave and not come back. I don't want to hear of you bothering these people." Red followed him, and soon the throaty rumble of the huge truck sounded through the house before growing quieter.

"Thanks, Red," Kyle said, still holding Mitzi. "I don't know what I'd do if we lost this little girl." He got kisses and then put her down. Mitzi raced to Hayden, and he patted her. Then she hurried to Red, as though eager to thank him herself. "Are you going to be able to do anything about him?"

"I have his plate and vehicle information. I'll talk to the chief and see if it's worth pursuing this further." He stroked Mitzi's head. "You be good for your daddies, little pumpkin. They both love you a lot." He smiled and set her down. Mitzi, having collected plenty of attention, hurried off to check out her bowl. Kyle gave her a treat, and she settled on the floor to munch it.

"I appreciate you coming," Hayden said. "Give our best to Terry. In the next couple of weeks, we should get together for dinner."

"Excellent idea. I'll send you a note with some times when we're available." Red shook both their hands before leaving the house.

"Red sure as hell got rid of him fast." Kyle chuckled softly. "How did you know?"

Hayden shrugged. "I think at the beginning it was more wishful thinking than anything else. I was hoping Mitzi wasn't his dog. But look at her—she loves everyone, yet she snapped at Gene. There was no way our little girl was his dog. And as for this sudden sister story, that just rang untrue as a giant lie that he had to come up with to explain Mitzi hating him." Hayden would do just about anything to protect his family. Hell, even before he fell in love with Kyle, he'd pulled him from a burning building, and now he'd saved Mitzi from an extortionist.

"Thank you for that," Kyle said.

Hayden pulled Kyle into an embrace. "Nothing to thank me for. Mitzi is part of us." He held Kyle tighter.

"Yes. She's our family." He held him equally tight. "Maybe you and I need to talk." He lifted his gaze. "I mean… you and Mitzi feel like part of the family. My family, the one I'm building. I know I have the one I was born into, but this isn't the same. It's the one we build ourselves." He barely paused for breath. "I heard once that lots of gay people build their own families because of the way their bio ones treat them. As a kid I guess I hoped that wouldn't happen to me, but it did. But you feel like my family."

Hayden smiled. "You feel like mine too."

Kyle nodded, and Hayden held his gaze. "So you'll stay here?"

Hayden's throat grew rough. "Are you asking me not to look for another apartment?" Hayden asked, and Kyle nodded.

"I want you and Mitzi to stay here with me because I love you. I'm crap at talking about my feelings and what I want. I think I just expect people to understand without words, and that's kind of dumb. How are you supposed to know what I want or how I feel if I don't tell you? No one can read minds, and—"

Hayden leaned forward and kissed Kyle. "How about we try to do better with that in the future? Because yes, I love you too. Not sure how it happened, but I do." Maybe it was the intensity of the way that he and Mitzi bonded. It could also have been the gentle way Kyle always treated him. Hayden rarely saw the remnants of the person Kyle had been in high school. That version of Kyle was long gone, and the man he was now was so much more.

"I don't want to keep thinking about how things were back in school. I didn't like the person I was then, and it took me a lot to become the man I am now."

Hayden brushed the hair away from Kyle's eyes. "I know that. The man you are now works for what he has, and he's so much more than that boy." Kyle didn't quite meet his gaze. "What's bothering you?" He knew Kyle well enough to have a sense about these things. Kyle would become quiet, and he'd bite his lower lip just slightly. He'd also knit his pinkies together. It was cute, but a sign of his worry.

Kyle swallowed. "You'll think it's stupid, and maybe it is. But I keep asking myself stuff, and you said all the right things just now. But can you really get beyond the past? Is it that easy?"

Hayden stared at first and then chuckled nervously. "No. It isn't easy. Those memories are still there, and they always will be." The cold, honest truth was what he had to express. "But they're different now. It's hard to explain, but I see things differently. See, when I remember back then, I see you as you were back then. I don't see you like you are now—the man. It was the boy Kyle who did that shit, and that's how I see it. I still don't like him. He was arrogant, scared, and a pure coward." Hayden felt the hurt from that period color his voice. "But when I look at you, the man in front of me now, I don't see him. I see you as you are. Grown, built, strong, and at the same time vulnerable. I like that."

"You like that I'm weak?" Kyle asked.

Hayden shook his head. "I didn't say weak. Vulnerable—there's a difference. Being vulnerable is showing that soft part of yourself and trusting that you won't be mistreated. It shows strength and character." He closed the distance between them. "It shows that you trust me enough to let me see that part of you. There's something sexy in not being perfect or having to be in control all the time."

"I see. And this part of me…?"

"Wasn't there in high school. You were all hard outer shell with nothing underneath. But you're different now, just like I am. I was too scared to stand up for myself then, and high school is a mess for everyone." Hayden decided to try another tack. "None of us are the people we'll become. So no, I don't see you the way you were then. Not any longer." He sighed and drew Kyle into his arms. "As I've said before, that's the past, and it can stay there, thank you very much. You, me, our dog, and the future are what we have to look forward to. I feel like it's up to us to see how we look at things." Hayden tilted Kyle's face upward and kissed him hard, letting his passion build. "And I look at you like this, well-kissed, eyes half-lidded, in my arms, content and happy. That's how I want to see you and how I think of you."

Kyle nodded slowly.

"Now, let's go on upstairs and see if we can't make the most of the start of the rest of our lives." He took Kyle's hand and turned out the lights as he led him up the stairs. They deserved to be happy, and Hayden intended to show Kyle just how amazingly happy they could be.

"JESUS. I THINK I'm going to feel you next week," Kyle whispered into the darkness. They were both covered in sweat, and Hayden had never felt better... or more completely wrung-out.

"Good. I want you to feel me and know that I'm with you even when I'm not there." He tugged him closer, positioning Kyle on top of him just so Hayden could feel his weight. "Love comes from places we never thought possible sometimes."

Kyle nodded. "I wish I had seen the possibilities a long time ago."

Hayden nuzzled him gently. "You see them now, and that's all that matters." He ran his hands down Kyle's back and over his smooth ass, loving the feeling and the way he shivered against him. "And I love you for it."

Kyle drew his head back slightly. "And I love you." He kissed Hayden hard, the heat building between them again. Kyle chuckled deeply, and Mitzi, who had jumped up on the bed once they had settled down, snorted and jumped off again, nails clicking on the wood floor. Sometimes that dog was too smart for her own good. Still, Hayden wasn't going to complain, not for a second. Hell, he intended to show Kyle how much he loved him all night long... and well into their future.

EPILOGUE

KYLE BOUNCED his leg on the floor, and Hayden went behind him and gently placed his hands on his shoulders. "There's nothing to be nervous about," Hayden said gently.

Kyle turned to look up at him, his eyes a little wild. "Are you kidding? I'm having lunch with my mother, brother, and sister. What the hell *isn't* there to be nervous about? Bella says that Mom wants to talk about Thanksgiving like we're some great big happy family."

"Hey. You've seen your mom and sister a few times over the past few months. This should be no big deal." Kyle and parts of his family had been repairing their broken relationship, but Kyle still wasn't ready to trust them. Not yet. And Hayden couldn't blame him. All he cared about was that Kyle was happy. "Let's get ready to go." Hayden gave Mitzi a treat and got her settled before getting their coats. He had suggested that they all meet at Café Belgie. It was a neutral location, and hopefully a public place would reduce the potential for drama.

Kyle stiffened his shoulders and shrugged on his coat. "Let's go." They went out to Hayden's truck, and he drove downtown.

"I have to ask—do you not want to spend Thanksgiving with your family?" Hayden asked. "My parents have invited us down to Florida to spend some time with them. Mom broached the subject when I spoke with her last week. I didn't give her an answer because I thought you might want to see your family for the holiday."

"Let's see how things go. Okay?" Kyle asked.

"Of course."

"Though a few days in Florida in November might be nice," Kyle commented as he turned, watching out the window as Hayden found a parking spot right in front of the restaurant. He parallel parked, and they got outside as light snow began falling. "I love this time of year, though it's a little early for snow."

"It's not supposed to be a lot." He locked the truck and walked with Kyle to the door of the restaurant. Kyle's family was already at a table, with two empty seats. Kyle paused just inside the door. "What is it?"

Kyle shrugged. "I guess I was hoping that Dad might have come, even though I knew he wouldn't," Kyle said softly before plastering a smile on his face as he strode to the table. He greeted his mother, Bella, and Jason before making reintroductions. Of course

Hayden knew Jason from work and couldn't help see-ing the scowl on his lips. Fortunately the reception from Bella and Kyle's mother was a different matter.

"Thank you both for coming," Kyle's mother said. She paused while the server took his and Kyle's drink orders. "I know things have been rough for a while."

Kyle took a drink from his water. "Let's not beat around the bush, Mom. Just say what you want to say and let's have it all out in the open." Hayden held Kyle's hand under the table.

"Fair enough. Your father cut you off, and the rest of us allowed that to happen. It was wrong. Your fa-ther is being an ass, and he can continue to do that if he wants, but the rest of us have decided to make up our own minds." Bella smiled, and their mom glared at Jason.

"I still say that if Kyle had acted faster, then Dad might be okay," Jason said.

"And you'd be wrong," Bella snapped back at him. "Stop being a stubborn jackass. Dad has kidney failure, and there is nothing Kyle or any of us can do about it. He wasn't any better a fit than either of us." Man, she could breathe fire when she wanted. Hayden liked Bella for that.

"It's time we all stop this," Kyle's mother said, her mouth pinched. "Your father and I are managing his health issues as best we can. But it isn't fair for any of us to put the blame on Kyle for that. We burned our bridges, and now it's up to us to try to repair them." She took Kyle's hand. "And I want to do that."

Kyle nodded, and Hayden squeezed his fingers gently. "What are your reservations?" Hayden asked.

"I keep waiting for the shoe to drop and everything to go back to the way it was," Kyle said levelly. "I'm not going to change who I am for any of you. Hayden and I are making our way together… as a family, and I love him." Kyle's voice was steady and strong. "If you can't deal with that, then he and I are going home and that's the end of it." He looked at Jason as he spoke.

"We all understand that," Bella said. "Don't we?" She joined the rest of the family in their glare-off.

"I get it," Jason grumbled. "I don't have to understand the whole gay thing. But Kyle's my brother. I'll figure out the rest."

"Good. Now, let's order some dinner, and then we can figure out what we're going to do for the holidays."

Kyle cleared his throat. "Hayden and I are going to see his family for Thanksgiving. They invited us down, and I've never met them. We're going to take Mitzi too, and she can play on the beach." He and Hayden shared a smile. "We'll be here for Christmas, and we can get together at some point." He didn't look away from Hayden. "But the one thing I want you all to know is that Hayden is my family." Kyle lifted their hands and placed them on the edge of the table.

"Kyle and I are going to make a life together." Hayden smiled and squeezed Kyle's fingers.

Kyle nodded. "So understand that if you want me in your life, it's us. Hayden and me. We'll come to Christmas, but it will be the two of us." Kyle looked around the table, but Hayden kept his gaze on Kyle. This was one of those moments of total bravery and love, and he wasn't going to miss any part of it.

"Of course," Kyle's mother said. "I'd expect nothing less." She smiled and reached across the table to place her hand on top of theirs. "You're my son." She patted their hands and then lifted hers away before catching the eye of their server. "We should order, and you can tell me all about what you've been doing."

This was not the dinner Hayden had been expecting, and it seemed it was a surprise to Kyle too.

"DO YOU really think she was on the level?" Kyle asked once they were back at the house, coats hung up, and sitting on the sofa. Mitzi took the place between them so she could get attention from both of them.

"Only time will tell," Hayden said. "But I have you, and you have me. We're a family." He leaned over and kissed Kyle gently, with Mitzi giving them both a lick. "Your mom and sister seem determined. Jason is probably on the fence, but I'm going to be here no matter what." He cuddled Kyle closer. "And the rest we'll figure out as we go."

"I like that. I just hope it doesn't take forever to know what's what."

Hayden cupped Kyle's cheek. "You and I have all the time in the world."

Kyle nodded. "And that's all that matters."

Hayden couldn't have said it better himself.

Keep reading for an excerpt from
Rekindled Flame
by Andrew Grey.

CHAPTER 1

THE ROAR and screech of the siren faded into the background as the truck slowed to a stop. Morgan popped his seat belt off and jumped down as the wheels quit rolling. Seconds mattered. He'd had that drilled into him since his first day of training, and it was now ingrained into his base personality. He was already pulling hoses off the back of the truck, laying them out as others hooked them up without a word. They knew exactly what to do. They'd practiced so many times they did their jobs without thinking about it.

"The upper floor is nearly completely engulfed. Get some water on it right away," the captain said even as the hose was connected and pressure began to build inside it.

Morgan turned to the group of people gathered in sleepwear toward the back of the lawn, huddled together. He hurried over as soon as the sound of water and fire mixing sent a hiss of steam into the air. "Is everyone out?" he asked them. They looked at each other, stunned.

"Richard isn't here," a kid in blue pajamas answered after a few seconds.

"Oh God," the woman, presumably the mother, groaned. "He lives in the small apartment." She pointed to the side addition of the compact house. "The door is right around the side."

"Thanks, ma'am," Morgan said and hurried back to the captain. "Someone is still inside. The family hasn't seen the tenant, Richard. I'm getting my breathing gear." He didn't wait for an answer as he pulled on a tank and mask with practiced ease. Time was of the essence. Even with the water that was being poured on the structure, the fire was still hot and doing its best to consume the old, dry home. He had a few seconds to ponder just why the house was going up so quickly before he was hurrying up the yard, water running down his suit to give him an initial layer of protection before he went in.

"Shit," he said into his communication system. "There's a ramp." He kicked open the side door. Blinding smoke poured out. Morgan hesitated for a second to give the worst of it the chance to escape before plunging into a world of danger.

The fire roared continually, even though he couldn't see it. The air was hot and getting hotter, which told him the fire was just on the other side of the walls and would most likely break through at any second. He scanned the small living area and then opened the first door he saw. It was empty of anyone as far as he could see. Morgan turned and pushed at another door. It didn't move. Without hesitating, he kicked it, sending the door flying inward.

A man sat in a wheelchair, slumped forward. Morgan had no time to assess his condition. The air was smoky and getting worse.

A crash sounded behind him, and the heat increased. Lights now danced on the walls of the other room. Morgan hefted the man into his arms and over his shoulder. Then he turned and left the room.

Flames crawled across the ceiling, heading for the same door as Morgan. It was a race: him to the exit and the fire to the source of air. Morgan walked as quickly as he could carrying the weight, the flames now racing throughout the room. He knew that within seconds his exit would be closed off.

A figure appeared in the doorway, and water shot to the side and above him, buying Morgan precious seconds that he was able to use to reach the door and safety. He stepped outside and down the ramp, heading right for the first ambulance he saw.

EMTs met him in the yard with a stretcher, and he laid Richard down on it as gently as he could and stepped back, hoping like hell he wasn't too late. Morgan took off his helmet and breathed, taking in cool, clear air. He was sweating like a pig and pulled open the latches of his fire coat to let some of the spring air inside. A bottle of water was shoved into his hand, and he drank without thinking, looking to where he'd left Richard and sighing with relief when he saw him with a breathing mask on. No CPR, just oxygen. He was breathing.

"You did good, again," the captain said, motioning him away from the others. "But this breakneck decision-making of yours has to stop," he added softly. "You ran in there before anyone could assess the situation." A crash interrupted them as the front wall of the home collapsed and fell inward. "You could have been inside."

"So could that man. Instead we're both outside and safe." He and the captain didn't see eye to eye on a number of things, least of which was the speed Morgan thought things needed to be done. The captain was too cautious and lost precious time, in his opinion. But he kept that to himself for now. "You know seconds count. We've all been taught that from day one. I used those seconds to rescue a man in a wheelchair." There was no way the captain could argue with that result.

"All right. It worked out this time, but what if you'd been caught inside?" he countered.

Morgan nodded and went back to work. Having an argument now wasn't going to get him anything, and the captain was worked up enough that if he pressed it, Morgan would find himself in front of the chief once again to explain why he'd done the right thing. It was getting annoying.

He went over to where the EMTs were loading Richard into the back of the ambulance. "Is he going to be all right?"

"He got way too much smoke, but we believe you got to him in time. He's already breathing somewhat better, and he's starting to come around, but he's still groggy and out of it. We're transporting him, but I suspect you saved his life."

"Thanks, Gary." Over time he'd gotten to know most of the ambulance drivers and EMTs. It was a hazard of the profession that their paths crossed too many times. They shook hands, and Morgan turned and went back to where the rest of the guys continued to pour water on what was left of the house, dousing the last of the flames.

By the time they started packing up, the Red Cross had arrived and was meeting with the family. Jackets had been provided, as had water and something to eat. Morgan knew from experience that they'd be helped with temporary shelter as well as given guidance for wading through dealing with insurance and trying to rebuild their lives.

Morgan walked to where they stood.

"Is Richard going to be okay?" the same young boy asked.

"We think so. They're going to take him to the hospital. Is he a family member?" Morgan asked.

"Sort of," the woman said. "He was in the same unit as my brother, Billy, and has been renting the apartment for the last year or so. The kids adore him and call him Uncle Rich, but he isn't a blood relation."

"Billy didn't make it home," the man standing with her explained, and Morgan nodded.

"He'll most likely be taken to Harrisburg Hospital. It's the closest, and they'll do everything they can for him. For now, get yourselves somewhere safe and warm for the night." The kids had to be getting cold in the night air, and he had work he had to do to help the other guys clean up. At times like this, he was never sure what to say, so he tipped his hat and joined the men draining the hoses to load them back on the trucks.

"That was something else," Henry Porter said, smile shining on his smoke-smudged face. "When I saw you coming out of that smoke, it was a damn miracle."

"You got there just in time," Morgan told the younger firefighter, returning his smile. "I wasn't certain I was going to make it until you bought me the time."

"You were going to make it, but I was glad to help." He was all smiles as they rolled up the hoses.

"I heard the guy was a veteran," Jimmy Connors said, gathering the nozzles and other equipment. "In a wheelchair."

"Apparently," Morgan said. "It was a good night. Everyone got out." He hated seeing the faces of families who had lost everything. They always seemed so haunted and unsure of what was going to happen next. Morgan had seen that in the family tonight, along with relief that Richard had been rescued safely.

"All right, let's get the last of this packed up so we can go back to the station," the captain called encouragingly, and their talking ceased as they all got to work. What could be pulled out and put to use in a matter of minutes always took much longer to stow and get ready for the next time it was needed. When the equipment was stowed and the area cleaned up, they climbed into the trucks and quietly went back to the station.

Morgan dragged himself off the truck. The energy that had sustained him at the fire and through the rescue had now deserted him, and all he wanted was to climb into a bed. Working late when most people are asleep was the hardest part of this job for him. Morgan was a morning person. At home he was usually up early, always had been, so working late into the night went counter to his natural rhythm.

"Let's get the hoses set to dry and call it a night. The rest can wait," the captain said, and the men got to work and then headed inside and up to the dormitory.

They often worked long shifts, and catching a few hours' sleep was always a godsend. Some of the guys would sit at the table and play cards or talk through the entire shift. Not Morgan. He headed right up and took his turn in the bathroom, then collapsed on one of the narrow beds, letting oblivion take over for a little while.

He only slept for a few hours, just long enough to recharge his batteries, and then he was up once again, helping to prepare the equipment for the next call, which they all knew could come at any moment.

"What will you do now that your rotation is over and you have some time off?" Henry asked without looking up from where he was cleaning the side of the pumper. The younger man's enthusiasm always seemed to run over the brim.

"I don't know. Probably sleep for a while, and then…." That was always the part of that answer that vexed him. Outside of work he didn't have much of a life.

"Will you go out, find someone to keep you company?" Henry waggled his eyebrows and reminded Morgan just how young Henry was and how old he seemed to be getting. "There are some great clubs downtown, and the girls would be more than interested, if you know what I mean. They love firemen."

"Is that why you became one?" Morgan asked. He was only giving Henry a hard time. Being a firefighter had to be in your blood or you didn't last very long. The job demanded a lot, physically, personally. It tended to take over and become what your life—well, at least his life—revolved around. Relationships suffered, and most went by the wayside over time.

"You know it's not," Henry answered seriously. "But it is one of the perks of the job."

Morgan paused. "You know you aren't likely to see me in one of those particular clubs." Morgan had decided some years earlier that he wasn't going to hide who he was.

"I thought that was only rumor and such." Henry looked him over. "You don't look like you're… that way." From what Henry had said and the way he'd talked sometimes, Morgan figured Henry had come to them straight off a rural Lancaster farm.

"Gay people come in all shapes and sizes, and believe it or not, we can do just about anything."

Henry's gaze drifted to the floor, hand stopping for a second. "I didn't mean anything by it. I guess you're just the first gay person I've met." He continued working.

"I don't think so. You remember Angus, the man who came in at the last training session talking about how fires start? He has a partner who isn't a woman. They've been together about a year now, I guess. His name's Kevin, and he's really nice."

"You know them?"

"I've met Kevin one time." Morgan didn't want to go into how all gay people didn't necessarily know each other. It wasn't his job to educate the kid, nor was it wise to try to pop too many of his bubbles all at once. "You okay?"

"Yeah," Henry answered quickly.

Morgan knew he was covering some discomfort, and Morgan figured that was okay. "If you've got questions, ask."

Henry wiped faster and faster. Soon Morgan figured either his arm was going to fall off or he was going to rub right through the red paint.

"There's no reason to be upset or nervous."

He finally stopped and set down the rag, working his arm in a circle because he must have made it sore. "But what if…." He stopped and shook his head. "I'm being dumb, right?"

"Maybe a little?" Morgan teased. "Now get back to work, and try not to rub all the paint off." He picked up another rag and helped the kid. Polishing was one of the most detailed and mind-numbing jobs, and usually it fell to the newbies. Morgan never minded it, and he could help the kid out. They were all a team.

Once his shift was over a few hours later, Morgan gathered his things to get ready to leave. There had been no further calls, and turnover to the morning shift had been completed. "You working today too?" Morgan asked Henry when he didn't seem to be getting ready to go.

"They're a man short, and I volunteered. They need the help, and I can use the hours."

"Don't wear yourself out. This job is a marathon that can last a long time." He clapped the young firefighter on the shoulder.

"Don't worry," Phillips, one of the senior firefighters, said. "We'll make sure he gets rest."

Morgan nodded and hefted his bag. "Are you going somewhere in particular?" Henry asked, following him out.

"Yeah, I'm going to stop at the hospital to see how the man I helped last night is doing, and then I'm going home." Morgan headed for the door and threw his bag into the trunk of his car before pulling out and driving across town to a place he knew way too well.

Morgan had saved a number of people over the years. It was one of the things that went with the job. Not getting there in time could rip a firefighter apart, and saving someone brought you a kinship no one else could understand. All he knew about this man was that his name was Richard, but in a few minutes they had shared something unique. Morgan had had an influence on the rest of Richard's life.

"Can I help you?" the woman behind the visitors' desk asked as he approached. "Oh, hi, Morgan," she said when she recognized him. "What can I do for you?"

"There was a man brought into emergency last night. His first name was Richard. I need to know what room he's in."

"You don't want much," she told him and began typing. Geri was used to his unorthodox inquiries. She was a little younger than him and had worked at the hospital for years. "What happened to him?"

"I got him out of a burning building last night, and I want to make sure he's okay." He leaned against the counter, relaxing while she searched.

"I found him. Room 212. It says he can receive visitors."

She handed him a pass, and Morgan thanked her before striding toward the elevators. He rode to the second floor and then walked through familiar hallways to the ward and down to Richard's room. He paused outside and heard nothing. Peering in, he saw a sleeping figure in the bed. Maybe he'd come too early. He walked in anyway and stood by the end of the bed.

"Who are you?" Richard demanded in a rough voice that set Morgan on alert.

"I'm the firefighter who pulled you out last night. I just wanted to make sure you were okay."

"You rescued me from the fire?" he asked. "You should have saved your efforts and left me there.

Everyone would be so much better off." The anger and vitriol rolled off him in a tidal wave of blackness.

"Well, I did," Morgan said as he put his jacket on the nearby chair. "The kids were worried about you."

That softened some of Richard's features as a nurse came rushing into the room. "Mr. Smalley, you need to remain calm." She helped him to lie back down, glaring at Morgan. "His breathing needs to be as regular as possible to give him time to heal."

Morgan barely heard her. He stared at the man in the bed and let her do her job. Once she left, he moved closer.

"Richard Smalley? Did you grow up on a farm outside Enola?" Even before Richard spoke, Morgan knew the answer.

"Yes." Richard lifted his head of sandy-blond hair, the color of perfectly ripe corn. Morgan knew that color so well, even after all these years.

"It's Morgan, Morgan Ayers. We were friends when we were growing up." He continued staring at the man Richie had become. "What were we, thirteen the last time we saw each other?"

"Yeah. After seventh grade when your dad moved the two of you away. Where did you go? I went away to summer camp, and when I came back you'd moved."

Morgan nodded. "Dad lost his job and got a new one in Detroit, so he packed us up and we moved. Not that we stayed there for very long either. After that we were in Cleveland, and then Pittsburgh, where Dad finally stopped drinking and we could settle down. He remarried, and that's where I spent my last few years of high school." God, he wanted to hurry forward and give Richard a hug, but he didn't have the right any longer. It had been decades, but Morgan had never forgotten Richie. How could he? "I wrote you, but I was thirteen and...."

"Yeah. It wasn't like there was Facebook back then."

Richard was definitely happier than he'd been, with a hint of the smile Morgan remembered from his friend. The memories had dulled over time as the years had gone by, but Morgan would never forget Richie, no matter how long he lived. That wasn't possible. How did you forget the one person you told your deepest, darkest secrets to, and he'd not only understood but told you his in return? How did you forget the boy who had made things better and brought you home when your dad drank most of the grocery money away? Richie had been the one who'd helped see that he didn't starve more times than he wanted to remember.

"You're a firefighter?" Richie asked. "You always said that was what you wanted to be when you grew up, even back then."

"Yeah, and it's a good thing I was, because I hauled you out of the bedroom last night."

"I thought I was dead. I got so disoriented I thought the bedroom door was the way out, and then after that I didn't have the lung power to do anything else. The door closed, and that's the last thing I remember."

"I broke it down and got you out of there, carried you out over my shoulder." He pulled the chair closer to the bed, moved his jacket, and sat down. "You were out of it, but I got you out in time, and once they get the smoke out, you should be good to go."

Richie yanked the covers to the side. "I'll never be good to go again, Morgan." He looked down at his legs. "The best I can do is wheel myself around, but I'm assuming my chair got fried."

"Along with everything else, I'm afraid. The fire was really hot, and I got you out just before it broke through. Damn thing chased me to the door." He wished he had better news.

"Did everyone else get out?" Richie asked.

"Yeah. They were pretty shaken up, and the Red Cross was helping them. But they were all okay."

"I served with Grace's brother in Iraq," Richie said.

"You always wanted to be a soldier," Morgan said. "Marine?"

"Yeah."

Richie looked totally pained, and he had to be wearing out. There were so many questions Morgan wanted to ask, but Richie was fading, and wearing him out wasn't going to do any good.

"I think I'm getting tired."

Morgan nodded and was about to stand up.

"You aren't going to disappear for a few decades again, are you?" Richie asked.

"No. I'm going to head home to get some rest since I just got off shift, but I'll stop by later today to make sure you're doing okay, and we can talk some more." Morgan stood and found a pen and pad on the tray. He jotted down his number for Richie. "I'll see you later."

They shared a smile, and then Richie's eyes drifted closed, so Morgan left the room.

He walked back through the hospital hallways in a slight daze, unable to believe he'd found his friend after all these years. By the time he made it to the exit, he was grinning like an idiot, and his spirit felt lighter than it had in a very long time. He had no logical reason to feel that way. But it didn't seem to matter.

He drove home humming to himself. He was fuck-ing *humming*. Morgan rarely hummed, sang, or whis-tled. He turned on the radio, and within moments he was singing along with the music. By the time he got home, Morgan was damn near giddy. And he was nev-er that happy or excited about much of anything. God, he was so pathetic. He worked, took care of his home, worked some more, and slept. That was his life, and it had been that way for so long he couldn't remember anything different.

Since he was a municipal employee of Harrisburg, he was required to live in the city. Luckily years ago he'd been able to buy a house in the Italian Lake neigh-borhood. It was one of the nicer areas of the city. He pulled his car into the garage and hoisted his bag of gear out of the trunk before heading inside.

Morgan dropped his gear in the foyer and contin-ued on through the house, where he checked the mail and took a few minutes to answer some emails before heading to the bathroom.

A shower, comfortable clothes, and a light blanket later, he was curled on the sofa, watching television and trying to relax. But all he kept thinking of was Richie and wondering what he'd been through. To say that Richie had been through a lot had to be an understate-ment. He knew there was something traumatic behind his inability to walk, but there was more than that. His reaction told Morgan that Richie didn't think he had much to live for, and that was really sad, because the Richie he remembered was pretty damned special.

ANDREW GREY is the author of more than one hundred works of Contemporary Gay Romantic fiction. After twenty-seven years in corporate America, he has now settled down in Central Pennsylvania with his husband of more than twenty-five years, Dominic, and his laptop. An interesting ménage. Andrew grew up in western Michigan with a father who loved to tell stories and a mother who loved to read them. Since then he has lived throughout the country and traveled throughout the world. He is a recipient of the RWA Centennial Award, has a master's degree from the University of Wisconsin–Milwaukee, and now writes full-time. Andrew's hobbies include collecting antiques, gardening, and leaving his dirty dishes anywhere but in the sink (particularly when writing). He considers himself blessed with an accepting family, fantastic friends, and the world's most supportive and loving partner. Andrew currently lives in beautiful, historic Carlisle, Pennsylvania.

Email: andrewgrey@comcast.net

Website:www.andrewgreybooks.com

Follow me on BookBub

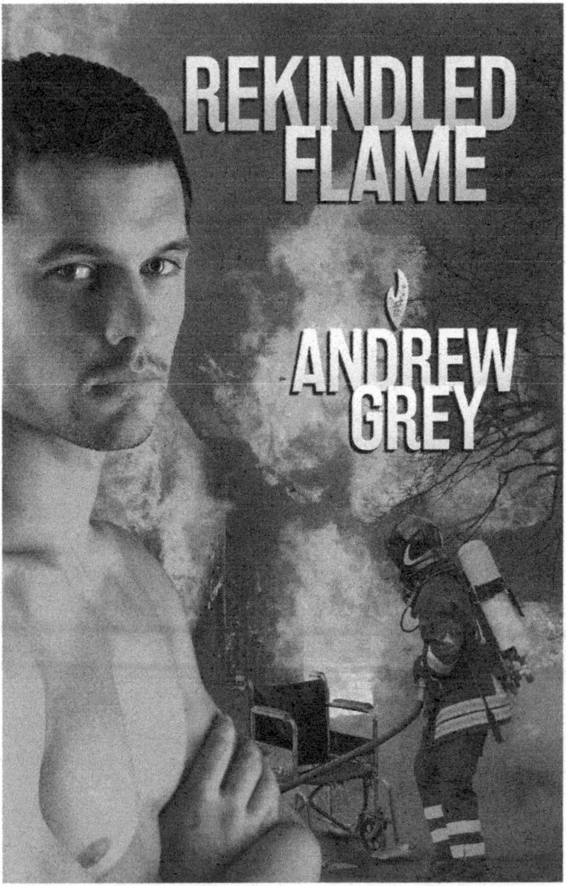
REKINDLED
FLAME
ANDREW
GREY

Rekindled Flame: Book One

Firefighter Morgan has worked hard to build a home for himself after a nomadic childhood. When Morgan is called to a fire, he finds the family out front, but their tenant still inside. He rescues Richard Smalley, who turns out to be an old friend he hasn't seen in years and the one person he regretted leaving behind.

Richard has had a hard life. He served in the military, where he lost the use of his legs, and has been struggling to make his way since coming home. Now that he no longer has a place to live, Morgan takes him in, but when someone attempts to set fire to Morgan's house, they both become suspicious and wonder what's going on.

Years ago Morgan was gutted when he moved away, leaving Richard behind, so he's happy to pick things up where they left off. But now that Richard seems to be the target of an arsonist, he may not be the safest person to be around.

www.dreamspinnerpress.com

CLEANSING
FLAME

ANDREW
GREY

Sequel to Rekindled Flame
Rekindled Flame: Book Two

Life has been grinding Dayne Mills down almost for as long as he can remember. First he lost the love of his life in an accident that also left him with a permanent injury, and then his mother passed away a year later. When his house burns to the ground, it's the last straw. He can't take any more, and if it wasn't for kind and handsome firefighter Lawson Martin offering him a hand up and a place to stay, he doesn't know what he'd do. Dayne would love for his relationship with Lawson to evolve into something beyond charity, but he knows going after a man so far out of his league will only lead to yet more heartache. It's best to just keep his mind on his research.

It's that research that leads Dayne to an old student journal that not only provides clues to the Native American heritage Lawson has been searching for, but chronicles a century-old love story. The tale that unfolds might be just what Dayne and Lawson need to remind them that no matter how dark life becomes, love can find a way to shine through.

www.dreamspinnerpress.com

SMOLDERING FLAME

ANDREW GREY

Rekindled Flame: Book Three

Sometimes the strongest flames take the longest to ignite.

Firefighter Dean's life revolves around his very ill son, Sammy. Caring for Sammy and working to make ends meet leave Dean time for little else, and romance isn't something he can even consider—no matter how much he longs for someone special to join their family. Because money is tight, Dean couldn't be more grateful to the photographer who does Sammy's session free of charge.

After growing up in the foster care system, Marco knows how to rely on himself, and his hard work is about to pay off—he's poised on the cusp of fame and success he could only have imagined as a lonely child. When Dean brings Sammy into Marco's studio, Marco can see they're struggling, and both the boy and his father stir Marco's heart. The slow burn between the two men isn't something either expected, but neither wants to lose the possibility of a loving future. With Dean's dangerous and possibly life-threatening career and Marco's demanding one, can romance and forever find a place to fit?

www.dreamspinnerpress.com

PAST HIS DEFENSES

ANDREW GREY

When a case reopens old wounds from the kidnapping of his younger sister, police officer Robert Fenner is told in no uncertain terms that he needs a break. And maybe his superiors are right. He books a flight to visit an old friend, who happens to be the one who got away, and hopes for the best.

Electronic security consultant Dixie Halewood works from his home in Paris, where he lives with his adopted son, Henri. Dixie doesn't expect a message from an old flame asking for a place to stay, but he agrees. Their past is just that—the past.

Things between them aren't as settled as they thought—Henri, Paris, and proximity work their magic. The two men are drawn closer and old flames burst back to life, but Dixie's work brings a new threat to their safety and the budding family they missed out on the first time around.

www.dreamspinnerpress.com

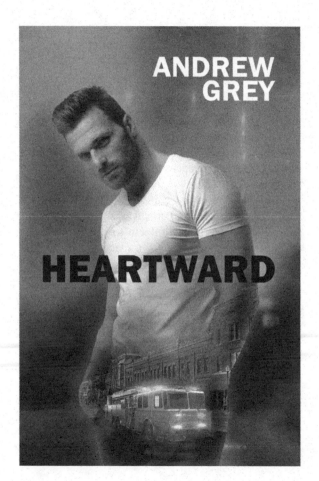

He doesn't know that home is where his heart will be....

Firefighter Tyler Banik has seen his share of adventure while working disaster relief with the Red Cross. But now that he's adopted Abey, he's ready to leave the danger behind and put down roots. That means returning to his hometown—where the last thing he anticipates is falling for his high school nemesis.

Alan Pettaprin isn't the boy he used to be. As a business owner and council member, he's working hard to improve life in Scottville for everyone. Nobody is more surprised than Alan when Tyler returns, but he's glad. For him, it's a chance to set things right. Little does he guess he and Tyler will find the missing pieces of themselves in each other. Old rivalries are left in the ashes, passion burns bright, and the possibility for a future together stretches in front of them....

But not everyone in town is glad to see Tyler return....

www.dreamspinnerpress.com